"To you, Katy." Alec raised his glass to hers.

Maybe it was because she couldn't see too well through the tears in her eyes, but for whatever reason, as she tried to clink her glass to his, she completely missed. And managed to toss most of her glass of wine straight onto his lap.

"Oh! I'm so sorry, Alec!" Katy leaped from her seat, grabbing her napkin to vigorously dab at the wine staining the bottom of his shirt, moving down to dab even harder at the biggest pool of liquid in a place he didn't want her dabbing.

Or maybe he did, because seeing her hands on his groin, feeling them pressing against him, shortened his breath, stepped up the beat of his heart, and invited an instant physical response he couldn't control.

"Let me handle it, Katy," he said, firmly grabbing her wrist before she could feel exactly what was happening to him and embarrass them both.

"But the stain is setting, and—oh!" Suddenly her motions stilled and her widening eyes met his. Obviously his body's response to her hands all over him was plenty clear.

"Yeah. *Oh.*" What else could he say? Except, maybe, *Touch me some more, please.*

Dear Reader

Have you ever been tempted by something you know might not be the wisest choice for you? That second piece of chocolate cake, or a few extra lottery tickets for that big jackpot, or maybe an item you want to buy but can't afford?

My heroine in this book, Katy Pappas, hero-worshipped her older brother's best friend Alec Armstrong. Until he disappointed her—twice—and she wrote him off. Now that she's graduated from medical school Katy has taken a job as a student intern at a hospital in beautiful San Diego, California. The same hospital where her brother and Alec both work as surgeons. As she begins to see the Alec she once believed him to be Katy finds herself drawn to him again. Except he's her teacher, and a relationship between them is strictly forbidden. Should she give in to temptation, risking her heart to a man with a past? A man who also happens to be completely off-limits?

Alec Armstrong made a mistake in his life he's determined not to repeat. Until Katy shows up and turns that conviction upside down. Risking his heart isn't the problem for Alec—but risking both their careers most definitely is!

I hope you enjoy Alec and Katy's story. Drop me a line through my website, www.robingianna.com, or on my Robin Gianna Facebook page. I'd love to hear from you!

Robin

FLIRTING WITH DR OFF-LIMITS

BY
ROBIN GIANNA

MILLS
BOON®

First published in Great Britain 2014
by Mills & Boon, an imprint of Harlequin (UK) Limited,
Large Print edition 2015
Eton House, 18-24 Paradise Road,
Richmond, Surrey, TW9 1SR

ISBN: 978-0-263-25470-9

Harlequin (UK) Limited's policy is to use papers that are natural, renewable and recyclable products and made from wood grown in sustainable forests. The logging and manufacturing processes conform to the legal environmental regulations of the country of origin.

Printed and bound in Great Britain
by CPI Antony Rowe, Chippenham, Wiltshire

After completing a degree in journalism, working in the advertising industry, then becoming a stay-at-home mum, **Robin Gianna** had what she calls her midlife awakening. She decided she wanted to write the romance novels she'd loved since her teens, and embarked on that quest by joining RWA, Central Ohio Fiction Writers, and working hard at learning the craft.

She loves sharing the journey with her characters, helping them through obstacles and problems to find their own happily-ever-afters. When not writing, Robin likes to create in her kitchen, dig in the dirt, and enjoy life with her tolerant husband, three great kids, drooling bulldog and grouchy Siamese cat.

To learn more about her work visit her website: www.robingianna.com

Recent titles by Robin Gianna:

THE LAST TEMPTATION OF DR DALTON
CHANGED BY HIS SON'S SMILE

**Praise for
Robin Gianna:**

'If you're looking for a story sweet but exciting, characters loving but cautious, a fan of Medicals or looking for a story to try to see if you like the medical genre, CHANGED BY HIS SON'S SMILE is the story for you! I would never have guessed Robin is a debut author: the story flowed brilliantly, the dialogue was believable and I was thoroughly engaged in the medical dramas.'
—*Contemporary Romance Reviews*

Dedication

This one's for you, Meta, as you well know!

Whether I just need your great advice or
I'm seriously panicking, you're always there
for me. I can't thank you enough for that.
You're the best! xoxo

Acknowledgements

A huge thank you to my agent, Cori Deyoe
of Three Seas Literary Agency,
for pulling me from the fires with this one.
I so appreciate your tremendous help
and steadfast encouragement.

Another big thank you
to my editor, Laurie Johnson,
for the wonderful suggestions to pull this book
together, and for your patience and support.
I truly appreciate it.

CHAPTER ONE

KATHERINE PAPPAS HOPED with all her heart that she'd been abducted by aliens. And that an extraterrestrial scientific experiment had sucked her brain dry.

After all, she'd much rather believe that the blankness of her mind throughout the night had been due to interplanetary interference and not because she'd just plain forgotten everything she'd ever learned in medical school. Exactly three weeks after she'd graduated. With a new job as a first-year intern at the same well-respected hospital as her hotshot surgeon brother.

Katy sucked in a calming breath. *You know this stuff. Just quit with the nerves and do the job you've been dreaming of doing forever.* She moved into a corner so no one, hopefully, would notice her until she felt ready to head to the first patient's room for morning rounds. After wiping her sweaty hands on her scrubs, she began to organize cards on each patient she'd be seeing that morning,

The shrill sound of her phone made her nearly jump out of her skin, and her stomach somehow both sank and knotted as she answered. The words that had been so wonderful to say just a week ago seemed to stick in her throat and choke her. "Dr. Pappas."

"Paging Dr. Katherine Pappas, world's best surgical intern on her way to becoming world's best family practice physician. Is she available?"

Hearing the voice of her closest friend in med school, Rachel Egan, made Katy relax and even conjure a small grin. "Dr. Pappas is available, except more likely she's on her way to becoming the first intern booted out of Oceancrest Community Hospital only hours after arriving."

"Uh-oh," Rachel said. "Bad night on call?"

"The nurses are probably referring to me as Dr. Dolittle. As in do very little." She sighed. "All night when they asked me questions, the right answer seemed to take a minute to percolate in my brain. I was sure I could do this, but now I'm worried."

"You're being ridiculous. Who had a straight four-point GPA in both undergrad and med school, like any human can do that? Who got the Alpha Omega Alpha award when we graduated? You're brilliant, Katy, and you're the only one who doesn't realize it."

"Then why doesn't the perfect answer pop instantly into my 'brilliant' brain?"

"Because we're nervous newbies, that's why. We crossed that med-school finish line, and all of a sudden we have the word 'Doctor' in front of our names and have to answer to it. Who wouldn't be scared? I know I am."

"Really? You are?" Rachel had always been the calm and confident student, the one who'd earned smiles and praise from professors and attending physicians for her cool and collected demeanor. In stark contrast to Katy's often ruffled one.

"Heck, yes, I am! I wish we'd ended up training at the same hospital. Maybe we'd both feel less freaked out if we had each other to lean on."

"I know. But you're happy to be back in your hometown, and I'm thrilled to be in San Diego. Plus I think it's good that I moved in with Nick. He's going through a hard time right now."

"Still pretty depressed about his divorce, huh?"

"Actually, the divorce isn't final yet. But, yeah, he's very glum compared to his usual self." Katy didn't know what had gone wrong in her brother's marriage, but it was sad that, after just a year, it hadn't worked out. She wished she could blame his wife, Meredith, except Katy had always liked her a lot—and, as the saying went, it took two to tango. Whatever their problems, both of them had probably contributed to them.

"It'll be good for him to have you there, I'm sure, though I hope nobody gossips about favoritism since you're his sister."

Favoritism? Katy hadn't even thought about that, and hopefully no one else would either.

"So, tell me—"

Katy's hospital call system buzzed and her belly tightened. "Gotta go, Rachel." She punched the button and swallowed hard before she tried to talk. "Dr. Pappas."

"Mrs. Patterson's potassium is at three point zero, and I need to know what you want me to do."

Okay, so that was low. She should order a potassium IV—probably four mil. No, wait. Maybe she should give it orally? A nervous laugh bubbled up in her throat as she wondered how the nurse would react if she prescribed a banana to bring up the patient's potassium.

She swallowed. "You know, I'll have to call you right back."

"Are you serious?" the nurse said in an annoyed and condescending tone. "Fine. I'll be waiting."

"Okay." Katy's face burned as she turned off her phone and wiped her hands, which were somehow sweaty and icy cold at the same time, on her scrubs again. She fumbled in her pocket for her Scut Monkey book. Rachel made fun of her that she infinitely preferred using it over trying to look things up on the internet. But her little book had helped her more than once, and she was determined to get this right.

Katy gnawed her lip and studied the little book.

Based on the patient's age, weight, and kidney function, it looked like she was right. Four ml potassium to drink would be the safest, most effective approach. Okay, good. As she tried to call the nurse back she dropped her phone on the hard floor, sending the plastic cover soaring across the room.

She groaned as she grabbed up the phone, relieved to see it was still working. Klutzy Katy. Why had she been plagued with some pitiful clumsiness gene, and why did it get worse when she was nervous? Graceful under fire she was not.

She called the nurses' station, surprised that a different nurse answered to take the oral potassium order. How many staff worked in this hospital? The number must be mind-boggling.

Right, time to get to rounds!

The patient card on the top of her pile read "Angela Roberts, Room 1073." She went to knock on the door, pausing to inhale a deep breath. This was it! Seeing her very first patient in person as a real doctor! Yes, she'd inherited all of them from the resident who'd already seen them, but still. The thought was nerve-racking but thrilling, too, and a big, spontaneous smile came on her face.

"Hello, Mrs. Roberts. I'm Dr. Pappas, your intern. How are you feeling?"

"I'm all right, dear. Wishing they could figure out my spells so I can get the gall-bladder surgery over with."

"We're working hard to figure that out." She warmed her stethoscope against her palm before examining the woman. "We're in the process of ruling out things like seizures or transient ischemic attacks, which are little mini-strokes."

"Strokes? I'm sure I would know if I'd had a stroke, dear."

"TIAs are so tiny you might not notice." Katy smiled, her chest a little buoyant as she thought about this puzzle they were solving.

"Well," Mrs. Roberts said, waving her hand, "I trust Dr. Armstrong to know what he's doing. Whatever he figures out is right, I'm sure. He's a lovely man."

Katy felt her smile slip and she forced it back up, at the same time avoiding rolling her eyes.

"No doubt Dr. Armstrong is an excellent surgeon."

And excellent at other things, too. Like giving fake excuses for not being with someone—breaking hearts in the process—then turning around and doing exactly that with someone else. Like having inappropriate hospital affairs that got other people fired. Fooling everyone who used to think he was wonderful in every way.

The old embarrassment and anger filled her chest again when she thought of how many years she'd hero-worshipped the man who didn't deserve it.

"And handsome! So good looking, like a doctor on TV. I'm sure a young thing like you can hardly resist a handsome surgeon like Dr. Armstrong."

"He's my superior here at the hospital, Mrs. Roberts." Long ago, she'd agreed. She'd thought everything about him gorgeous—his football-player physique, his warm amber eyes, his thick dark hair. Funny and smart, with a teasing grin that was irresistible.

But no more. A man had to be beautiful on the inside as well as the outside to appeal to her. Not that she appealed to him anyway, which he'd made abundantly clear.

"I'm feeling a little tired." The woman snuggled down into her bed as Katy continued her examination. "Can you come back later?"

"I'm almost done for now, Mrs. Roberts. May I pull your sheet down a little? I just want to take a listen to your belly."

Katy glanced up when she didn't respond and was startled to see that her head had lolled to one side of the pillow, her mouth slack and her eyes closed. Had she fallen asleep, just like that?

"Mrs. Roberts?" Katy's heart sped up and she spoke louder, shaking the woman's shoulder. "Mrs. Roberts?"

The monitor the patient was hooked up to began to screech and Katy looked at the screen. Her oxygen level was dangerously low, but there was no change in her heart rate. That couldn't be right, could it? Quickly, she rubbed her knuckles against Mrs. Roberts's sternum.

Nothing. No response. Katy put shaky fingers

against the woman's carotid artery. Her pulse was so slow and faint Katy knew this was beyond serious. Heart pounding in her ears now, she leaped up and smacked the red code button on the wall then ran back to the bedside.

"Okay, Katy, you've got this," she said out loud to herself as her mind spun through the advanced cardiac life support protocol she'd finished during orientation just yesterday. "It's as easy as ABC, right? Airway, breathing, circulation."

Her own breath seriously short and choppy, she shoved the pillows from the bed to get Mrs. Roberts lying flat and lifted her chin to open her airway. The woman's chest still barely moved.

Damn it! Katy knew she had to get a bag valve mask on her immediately, then noticed the EKG wires had been disconnected, probably when she'd gone to the bathroom. Stay calm here, you know what to do, she reminded herself, sucking in a deep breath to keep from fainting along with Mrs. Roberts.

Fumbling with the equipment, she managed to stay focused as two nurses ran into the room.

"We need to get her back on the monitor. I need to bag her. Can you get me a bag valve mask? And another IV." She could practically smell their alarm and forced down her own. *Do not panic, Katy. This woman's life could depend on you.*

The loud sound of a cart rumbling down the hall and into the room made Katy sag in relief. The cavalry had arrived.

"Give me the patient's history," a guy said, as he moved from the crash cart to the head of the bed, quickly getting a bag on Mrs. Roberts to provide the oxygen she desperately needed. He was probably from the ICU team, but Katy wasn't about to waste time asking questions.

"Patient is eighty-two, with cholecystitis, her surgery is on hold until she's medically cleared by Cardiology." Katy gulped as she stared at the still-unresponsive Mrs. Roberts and forged on. "She was talking to me and just kind of collapsed. She has fainting spells and we're trying to figure out why."

She stared at the monitor as the ICU guy attached the last EKG lead. Involuntarily, Katy let out a little stressed cry when she saw the heart rate was alarmingly slow at only thirty-five beats per minute. "Sinus bradycardia," she said. "Atropine point five milligrams and we need pads for transcutaneous pacing."

Had all that really come right out of her mouth? No time to give herself a pat on the back as the ICU guy barked to the nurse, "Get Cardiology on the line. You, Doctor, get her paced as I intubate."

Katy blinked and a touch of panic welled in her chest that she resolutely tamped down. He'd just called her "Doctor". She was part of this team, which would hopefully save this woman's life. Concentrating intently on getting the pads placed amid a flurry of activity by the nurses, she didn't even notice the tall, broad form that came to stand next to her.

"I'll take over now," a familiar deep voice said. "Good job, Dr. Pappas."

Alec Armstrong brushed past her as she moved to one side, allowing him to deliver the electricity to Mrs. Roberts's heart. Katy stood there, stunned, her hands now shaking like a tambourine. Beyond glad it wasn't her trying to get the pacing finished and giving orders to the nurses.

Which wasn't the right attitude, she scolded herself, since she wanted to be a doctor—was a doctor. But, dang it, how many newbies had to deal with their very first patient coding on them?

She watched Alec work, and couldn't help but notice how different he was, and yet somehow the same as when she'd known him years ago. As a boy and teen, he'd practically lived in their house as Nick's best friend. While he'd been as fun and adventurous as anybody she'd known, he'd always become calm and focused when there had been an important task at hand, his eyes intent, just like they were now. His hands moved swiftly and efficiently, as they had during all the crazy science experiments they'd done together. All the times he and Nick had worked on projects with her, teasing about her endless quest to learn new things and solve weird problems.

Her hero-worship of Alec was over. But the moment that thought came into her head, as she watched him work, she knew it wasn't true. How could she not admire how capably he dealt with a critical situation? But she didn't have to like him as a person to admire how good he was as a doctor and doubtless as a surgeon.

In a short time the frantic flurry of activity was over and the ICU guy began to wheel Mrs. Roberts from the room. As he left, he said over his shoulder, "I'll dictate my procedure note. You got the code note?"

"I've got it," Katy and Alec said at the same time. Their eyes met, his the amused, warm amber she remembered so well, and she felt her face flush. How could she have thought the guy was talking to her when attending surgeon extraordinaire Alec Armstrong had taken over?

"So, Katy-Did." His lips curved as he folded his arms across his chest. "What the hell did you do to my patient to make her code like that?"

"Please call me Katherine or Katy. I'm not a kid anymore," she said with dignity. Which he should know after her ill-advised behavior at her brother James's wedding five years ago. Her cheeks burned hotter at the memory.

"Fine, Dr. Katherine Pappas." His smile broadened, showing his white teeth. "How did you almost kill her?"

"I didn't almost kill her, and you know it. I didn't do anything." Katy's voice rose to practically a squeak on the last word and she cleared her throat, forcing herself to sound somewhat professional. "I was talking with her and giving her an exam, and she just fainted. I think she probably has sick sinus syndrome, which is why she's sometimes fine and other times faints."

"Do you, now?" He laughed. Actually laughed, and Katy felt her face heat again, but this time in annoyance.

"Yes, I do. I may be a total newbie, but I'm allowed to give my opinion, aren't I? Isn't it part of my training to form an opinion, even if it's wrong?"

"It is. And you are. Right, I mean, not wrong. And why am I not surprised that on your first day you've figured out this woman's likely diagnosis?" He stepped closer, touching his fingertip to her forehead and giving it a few little taps. "Some things never change, and one of them is that amazing, analytical brain of yours."

Some things never changed? Wasn't that the unfortunate truth? In spite of him making clear he had no interest in her as a woman, in spite of everything she knew about the kind of man he was, being so close to Alec made her breath a little short, which irritated her even more. How was it possible that the deepest corners of her brain still clung to the youthful crush she used to have? But being on Dr. Playboy's teaching service for the next month would most definitely squelch the final remnants of that for good. She was sure of it.

His fingertip slipped to her temple then dropped away. "Teaching rounds begin in an hour. Not too many people get to brag about dealing with a code on their very first day." That crooked grin stayed on his mouth as he gave her a little wink. "You did great. Welcome to Oceancrest, Katy-Did."

He turned and walked from the room, and she found herself staring at his back. Noticing that his thick dark hair was slightly longer than the last time she'd seen him. Noticing how unbelievably great his butt looked in those scrubs, how his shoulders filled every inch of the green fabric.

Noticing how horribly unkempt she herself looked at that moment. She looked down at her own wrinkled scrubs before she glanced in Mrs. Roberts's bathroom mirror at circles under her eyes the size of an IV bag. Ridiculously messy hair that had been finger-combed at best and now looked like it had been tamed by an eggbeater. Sleeping in the on-call room—if you could call the few hours her eyes had been closed sleeping—did not exactly lend itself to looking pulled together and rested.

She sighed and ran her fingers through her hair. Why did it have to be that the first time Alec saw her at the hospital, she looked like a wreck?

And why did she care, anyway? The man was a player through and through.

Never would Alec have guessed he'd some-day have Katy Pappas on his surgical teaching service. The cute but clumsy little girl who'd bugged the hell out of him and her brother Nick when they'd been young, tagging along on their adventures and asking nonstop questions, for some reason believing they'd know the answers.

The worshipful gaze of her blue eyes had always made his chest puff up a little with pride. Despite how much he and Nick had complained about her hanging out with them, he'd always secretly liked it when she had. That someone had thought he was smart and worthy of that kind of adulation had felt damned good, since it had been in very short supply in his own home.

The nonstop criticism his father had doled out had made Alec want to live up—or down—to his father's expectations of him. He'd worked as hard at partying as he had at football, and probably the only reason he hadn't gone down in flames had been because he'd had the steady support of the Pappas family, and Dr. George Pappas in particular.

After he and Nick had headed off to college and medical school, he hadn't seen the Pappas clan again until five years ago at a family wedding. Gobsmacked that Katy, awkwardly geeky child and studious teenager, had morphed into a drop-dead gorgeous twenty-one-year-old woman, he remembered standing stock-still, staring at her in disbelief. Shocked that he'd found her attractive in a way that was *not* at all brotherly.

He'd been even more shocked when, standing in a quiet corner at the reception, a champagne-tipsy Katy had grabbed his face between her hands and pressed her mouth to his. A mouth so warm and soft and delectable that every synapse in his brain had short-circuited and he'd found himself kissing her back. Their lips had parted and tongues had danced as he'd sunk deeply into the mind-boggling pleasure of it.

Then sanity had returned and he'd practically pushed her away, horrified. No way could he have anything like that with Katy Pappas, little sister of his best friend. She was totally off-limits. Period.

He'd tried to make a joke of it. Katy, however, hadn't thought it was remotely amusing when he'd told her he didn't feel that way about her, and that it would be all wrong if he did.

If she'd been pressed closer against him, she

would have known part of that statement was a lie. But appropriate? Hell, no.

He sighed. From that moment on his friendship with Katy had been pretty much over. She'd been cool at other family functions since then. Aloof, even.

Alec had shoved down his feelings of disappointment that she was no longer the Katy who'd thought he was great. Hell, after the mess he'd made of some things in his life, he shouldn't expect anyone to feel that way.

Then he'd walked into the coding patient's room and seen her, wrinkled, messy, and nervous. Beautifully messy and nervous, yes, but so much like the Katy he'd once known he hadn't been able to help but want that old friendship back.

And just like the old Katy, in the midst of all the chaos she'd still shown what a brainiac she was. That she was good at figuring out what to do in any circumstances, despite being brand new at the art and science of doctoring.

Maybe it was absurd, pathetic even, but he wanted to see again the Katy who used to like and admire him, who had tolerated and even enjoyed his teasing.

Alec remembered well the feel of her lips against his. But a woman like her no doubt had so many boyfriends that a little kiss five years ago would have been completely forgotten.

CHAPTER TWO

As ALEC STRODE down the hall, he could see the residents and interns waiting for him at the end of it, but his gaze stuck fast on Katy.

She'd changed into street clothes and a lab coat, and had obviously found a minute to brush her hair, which was no longer in a tangle but instead covered her shoulders in lustrous waves. He remembered that thick hair of hers always falling into her eyes and face as they'd studied things together, and he'd gotten into the habit of tucking its softness behind her ears so she'd been able to see whatever he and Nick had been showing her.

Her hands waving around as she spoke—another thing that was such a part of who she was—Katy was talking intently to the young man next to her, a frown creasing her brows, which made Alec smile. If he had to guess, she was regaling the other new intern with details about some condition or patient she was wondering about, because that brain of hers never rested.

"Good morning, everyone. I'm Dr. Alec Armstrong, as most of you know." He forced his attention from Katy to look at the young man she was speaking with. "You must be Michael Coffman, one of our new interns. We're glad you're here. Please tell us about yourself."

"I'm going into general surgery, planning to specialize in urology."

"Excellent. Our other intern here is Katy Pappas." He smiled at her, but she just gave a small nod in return. "Tell us about your intended specialty."

"I'm going into family practice medicine. I really enjoyed working with all kinds of people during med school." She looked at the group around her and her expression warmed. "Older folks and little ones and everybody in between. Figuring out what their medical problems are, when sometimes it can be a bit of a mystery, fascinates me. Knowing I'm helping individuals and families alike. I'm going to love doing that kind of work."

She spoke fast, her blue eyes now sparkling with the enthusiasm he remembered from their childhood whenever she had been tackling a puzzle or been deep into a science project, and his own smile grew.

"I'm glad you've discovered your calling. Figuring that out is sometimes the hardest part of medical school." He found himself wanting to keep looking at her, wanting to hear her speak and see her smile, but he made himself turn to the rest of the group.

"So let's continue our introductions. This is our fifth-year surgical resident, Elizabeth Stark, who performed some of the surgeries on the patients we'll see this morning. You met our second-year surgical resident, Todd Eiterman, this morning on work rounds."

Alec finished the spiel he always gave new interns, hoping they actually listened. "Beyond the nuts and bolts of diagnosis and surgery I want to teach you how to talk to people, to ask questions and listen carefully to the answers, which is the only way to truly learn their histories. Conclude what you think the working diagnosis might be then order tests based on those conclusions."

"Excuse me, Dr. Armstrong, but last month Dr. Hillenbrand said the opposite, so I'm confused," Todd, the second-year resident, said with a frown. "I thought we were to order tests then, based on those tests, come up with a working diagnosis."

"Technology is an amazing thing, Todd. But it can't replace hands-on doctoring, which is the single most important thing I want you to learn on my rotation." Alec studied the expressions on the faces before him. Smug understanding from Elizabeth, who'd heard it more times from him than she wanted to, he was sure, and also liked to play suck-up to the doctor evaluating her. Skepticism from Todd. Bewilderment and confusion from Michael. And avid concentration and focus from Katy's big blue eyes, which made him wish he could pin a gold star on her before rounds had even begun.

The thought sent his gaze to the lapels of her coat and the V of smooth, golden skin showing above her silky blouse, and he quickly shifted his attention to Todd. She was his student, damn it. And perhaps someday again his friend. But thinking of her as a very attractive woman? An absolute no-no.

"We'll be seeing patients who had surgery the past couple of days," he continued, keeping his eyes off Katy. "But first we'll see Mrs. Patterson, on whom tests were run yesterday. I know you've made your work rounds, so a lot of what I'm going to say will be a repeat of what you already know."

Alec led the way toward Helen Patterson's room with the group of students following behind. Katy was closest to him, and her light, fresh scent seemed to waft to him, around him, pleasing his nostrils so much he picked up the pace to put another foot or so between them.

What kind of doctor was distracted by someone's sex appeal while in the middle of work? Not the kind of doctor he demanded he be, that was for sure. Not the kind of doctor he'd been at one time, long ago when he'd been younger and stupid.

"Dr. Pappas, will you tell me about this patient from your work rounds this morning?"

"This is Mrs. Helen Patterson, and she has been in a rehabilitation nursing facility for one week, post-op after surgery for a broken hip," Katy said. "She was admitted here yesterday for abdominal pain and referred to the surgery service. She had low blood pressure and her lactate was elevated."

Katy licked her lips nervously, and Alec yanked his gaze away from them. He tried to simply listen and not notice the serious blue of her eyes as she spoke. "We ordered a CT scan of her belly, and there was no evidence of perforation in the bowel or appendicitis. We observed her overnight, gave her IV fluids and pain meds and she has spontaneously improved. We've determined that she has a mild case of ischemic colitis. She had a normal breakfast, and her physical exam is normal, so she can be released today."

Her expression was both pleased and slightly anxious, and Alec hoped he wouldn't have to remind her about the low potassium he'd read about in Mrs. Patterson's chart, and that the repeat potassium was still slightly low. "And?"

"And her potassium was low this morning, but I gave orders that brought it up."

"Except that those orders were all wrong, Dr. Pappas," Elizabeth said. She had on her usual superior smirk that Alec had tried, with limited success, to get her to tone down when talking to less-experienced students. "You gave her forty mils to drink, which is way too much to give orally. How did you expect someone to drink that amount? I can only imagine how nasty it tasted to poor Mrs. Patterson. No surprise that she vomited it up and had to be given some intravenously to replace it."

Katy's smile froze, and all color seeped from her face, then surged back to fill her light olive skin with a deep rose flush. "What...? I... Oh. Oh, no! I didn't order forty mil. I ordered four ml!"

"Really?" Elizabeth raised her eyebrows. "Nurses sometimes mishear an order, but it's still your responsibility—"

To Alec's shock, Katy turned and tore into the

patient's room, and he quickly followed. What in the world was she doing?

She slid to the side of the patient's bed and reached for the woman's hand. Katy's expression was the absolute picture of remorse. "Helen, I didn't know it was my fault you got sick to your stomach this morning. I feel terrible! I guess the nurse misheard me and gave you way too much to drink. That's why you vomited. I'm so, so sorry."

Alec was torn between being impressed that she instantly took responsibility for what technically wasn't her mistake, and concern that the patient might get angry and let loose on her. He stood next to Katy, placed his hand on her back to let her know he was there to support her. "It's unfortunate that orders get confused sometimes, Mrs. Patterson. You're feeling okay now, though, aren't you?"

"Yes, it was just an upset stomach. Don't be angry with dear, lovely Dr. Pappas, now. She's such a good doctor. Everyone makes mistakes once in a while."

Dear, lovely Dr. Pappas? Alec smiled in relief. Obviously, the woman liked Katy and wasn't going to create a stink about the error. He glanced at the residents standing at the end of the bed and almost laughed at the variety of expressions on their faces. Michael was wide-eyed, Todd scowling, and Elizabeth fuming. Having been raked over the proverbial coals often during their training, the two more experienced doctors had obviously been hoping for the same for Katy.

"I'm glad you're feeling better." He looked at Katy and, luckily, she understood that he wanted her to stop holding the woman's hand and stand next to him in a more professional manner.

"Helen, as you can see, I have some interns and residents here with me this morning. Is it all right if they stay while we talk?"

"Of course, that's fine."

"Thank you." He proceeded to ask her questions and explain tests that were run, while palpating her abdomen and listening to her heart and lungs. In the midst of it she held up her hand and interrupted.

"Wait a minute." Helen frowned at him. "First,

why don't you warm up that stethoscope before you press it on my skin, like Dr. Pappas always does? That thing is cold!" She shifted her attention to Katy. "And why is he asking me the same things you asked me already, dear? Don't you two talk to each other?"

Katy laughed a little, and glanced at him with a smile in her eyes that felt like old times, making him smile, too. "It's just how it's done when we're being taught by the attending physician, Helen. I know it's kind of annoying but Dr. Armstrong is an amazing surgeon. I promise you're in good hands."

How absurd that her words, which were just to reassure the patient, made him almost feel like puffing up his chest just like the teen Alec who'd always appreciated her faith in him. Helen nodded and waved her hand. "Fine. Carry on."

"I appreciate the endorsement, Dr. Pappas." Alec could hear warmth creeping into his voice as he spoke and concentrated on cooling it. On sounding professional and impartial.

Katherine Pappas was his best friend's little sister and his own student. He had to make sure no one thought they saw any kind of favoritism in the way he interacted with her.

The term "bone-tired" took on a whole new meaning after all-night call with minimal sleep followed by a long day of rounding and scut work. Katy thought she'd worked long and hard in med school, but that had been a veritable party compared to this.

As she stepped through the front door into Nick's living room, he emerged from the kitchen. "Katy-Did, you're finally home! You look beat."

"Now, there's a surprise. I'm sure I look every bit as hot, sweaty, and wrinkled as I feel."

"Living hot, sweaty, and wrinkled is an intern's existence pretty much. Sometimes it's a general surgeon's existence, too." Nick grinned. "I knew you'd be exhausted, so I'm fixing dinner. You don't have to do a thing."

"Aw, you're the sweetest big brother anyone could ever have." She gave him a quick hug, hoping she didn't smell too bad. "What are we eating?"

"Steaks from the grill, baked potatoes, veg-

ROBIN GIANNA

gies. To celebrate your first day, and because you probably need iron and protein after practically twenty-four hours of work. How did it go, rounding with Alec?"

"He's a good teacher, of course. I'm sure I'll learn a lot from him." She dropped into a chair in Nick's living room because she thought her legs just might give out if she was on her feet another minute. "But you know how I feel about him personally."

"Katy." Her brother's smile faded. "Alec is a good guy, and I regret that I ever told you what happened. Yes, he went through a hellion stage when there was too much partying and too many of the wrong kinds of women in his life, but that was a long time ago. You need to cut him some slack."

"Why? He's not the person I thought he was. I'm allowed to be bothered by that, aren't I?"

"You thought he was cool and smart and cared about other people. You liked him because he treated you great. And that's exactly who he is, along with older and wiser than he was back then. Hell, I'm still working on the older and wiser part."

"Don't worry, I'm not going to be unpleasant or anything. I just don't want to be friends with him again, that's all."

"Well, that's too bad. Just remember he's still my friend. And a partner in my practice." He frowned at her for a moment then sighed. "You never really knew that Alec's dad was always putting him down, and I think that's part of why he acted out some back then. But for a long time now he's worked hard to gain respect. It's important to him. While he never did get it from his dad, he has it in spades from everyone here."

"I'm sure he's a good doctor, so of course people respect him."

"It's more than that, but I'm not going to waste my breath trying to convince you." He turned toward the kitchen. "I'm going to get the steaks on the grill and play with the dogs out in the yard. I'll let you know when it's ready."

He disappeared, and she stayed slumped in the chair, closing her eyes. Which made ignoring the mess of stuff she'd left lying around the room, still packed and unorganized, much easier. She knew she should work on it right now since Nick was being so sweet about letting her live with him for a while, but she also knew he was happy to let her rest a moment.

Much as he'd teased her over the years, Nick had been good to her, too. All six of the Pappas kids were, in fact, close, which Katy was more than thankful for. As an only child, she knew Alec had never had a sibling that he fought with sometimes but who also always had his back, and she knew that had been a big part of why he'd been at their house so much. Her mother had welcomed him, and her dad had adored and mentored him.

Which was why learning of his unethical and distasteful behavior had cut Katy to her very core. Not only that, Alec's parents had shoved what he'd done under a rug then wrapped it up with a nice tidy bow while someone else had paid the price.

Ah, who was she kidding? It hadn't been just his mistake and the aftermath that remained stuck as a sharp barb in her soul. It was that he'd done it all practically right after she'd boldly kissed him and he'd pushed her away. Told her it wouldn't be "appropriate." Which obviously had just been another way of saying, *I think of you as a little sister, not a woman*, since "appropriate" clearly hadn't entered his mind before the scandal.

Her chest burned in embarrassment and disgust but at the same time she couldn't deny that the man was an impressive doctor and teacher. And, yes, even more ridiculously good looking than he'd been years ago. Today, in Mrs. Patterson's room, as they'd smiled together at the woman's comments, she had to admit it had felt nice. A little like old times, and thoughts of his past had momentarily faded from her brain until she'd sternly reminded herself.

She was smart enough to take advantage of his intelligence and experience and learn what she could from him, just as she had long ago. But as far as a friendship happening between them again? Never.

The doorbell rang and, still collapsed in the chair, she nearly groaned. The last thing she wanted to do was talk to anyone. Maybe if she ignored it, whoever it was would go away.

The bell rang again and with a resigned sigh she shoved herself from the chair and forced herself to open the door.

To her shock, Alec stood there, looking annoyingly handsome in jeans and a yellow polo shirt that showed off his broad shoulders. Sunglasses covered his eyes. The evening sun gleamed in his dark hair and his admittedly attractive lips were curved in a smile that no doubt had women flocking around him like seagulls. And yet again she looked like she'd been through the heavy-duty wash cycle and hung out to dry.

What was Alec doing here?

"Hello, Dr. Armstrong. What can I do for you?"

His dark eyebrows rose as he slipped off his sunglasses. "Oh, so formal. What happened to the old 'Hi Alec, come on in' you used to greet me with?"

How was she supposed to answer that? She wanted to say that had been back when she'd been young and naive and worn rose-colored glasses, but there was no point in going there. "I wasn't sure if I should call you Alec, as you're an attending and I'm a student."

"It's fine for you to call me Alec when we're not in the hospital. Unless you particularly like guys in scrubs and want to call me 'Doctor.'" The teasing grin he gave her was downright dazzling, and she turned away from its power, opening the door fully as she doubted he'd stopped by just to say hello then leave.

"Funny. Though perhaps you're saying that because I know that you particularly like women in scrubs. Or, even more, in nothing at all."

Crap, had she actually just said that? Her cheeks burned and she couldn't figure out what part of the room to focus on, because she sure as heck wasn't going to look at him now. She quickly walked over to the pile of stuff she'd pulled out of a box and left on the sofa yesterday.

"Katy Pappas, I'm shocked that you—"

"Sorry the place is a bit of a mess," she interrupted, the deeply amused rumble of his voice making her blush all over again. She did not want to hear whatever he'd been about to say in response to her extremely ill-advised comment. She grabbed up her things and shoved them back in the box. "I haven't had time to put away all my stuff yet."

"Don't worry, I saw the housekeeping police are busy a few blocks away. I think you're safe until tomorrow."

His voice still held laughter and she focused on the box. Not. Going. To look at him. "As you can see, I haven't had a chance to change my clothes. Excuse me while—"

Excited woofs drowned out her words as Nick's two yellow Labrador retrievers bounded through the house to greet Alec, slamming against Katy and nearly knocking her off her feet. "Whoa!" she yelped, her tired legs not quite balancing the way they should. Before she tumbled to the floor Alec lunged to grab her and hold her upright, flattening her tight against him.

Her hands slapped up against his muscular shoulders as the feel of his firm chest against her breasts, his strong arms around her sent her breathing haywire. Their eyes met, and the grin faded from his, replaced by what looked like a slightly confused frown.

The seconds ticked by and both stood motionless, oddly frozen, until Katy grabbed what wits she had left. She pushed against his shoulders and stepped back as his arms dropped to his sides, but their gazes remained locked. The tingling of her nerves and the imprint of his body that she could still feel against her own must be some sort of "muscle memory" thing, from the years she'd written in her journal about how much she wanted to be held close by Alec.

"I see you still have a little clumsiness problem."

Her gaze moved from the oddly disturbing eye contact to his lips, which disturbed her in a different way. She looked down at the dogs for a distraction. "I don't think being knocked into by these crazy pups of his makes me clumsy," she said, hoping she didn't sound as breathless as she felt. The dogs wagged their tails and rubbed against her for attention, leaving dog hair all over her black skirt. As if she wasn't already enough of a mess. "Nick can't have much company—they've acted like this every time someone comes to the door. If they hadn't been outside, we would have been mauled the second you came in."

"They're still young and rambunctious." He looked oddly serious, considering his teasing of just a moment ago. "And in case you don't remember, your dogs pretty much all acted this way at your family's house. I remember your mutt, Buddy, chewing up one of my shoes that I'd left at the door."

She looked up at him as she scratched the dogs' heads. "You had to put up with a lot at our house, didn't you? Utter chaos, with six crazy kids and badly behaved dogs."

"I think the term would be bedlam." The smile was back on his face, and why she was pleased to see it again she wasn't sure. "But I enjoyed every minute of the time I spent with Nick. And you. And the rest of your family, of course."

"You two sitting out there, socializing, with your feet up?" Nick's voice called from the kitchen. "Katy has the night off, but you don't, Alec. I need a hand here."

"Coming in a sec. Just realized I left the wine I brought in the car." His index finger reached out to give her nose a gentle flick, a soft stroke from between her brows to its tip as he'd done more times than she could possibly count, but the expression in his eyes seemed different than in the past. Hotter, more intimate, somehow, and her heart stupidly sped up in response.

Thankfully, he turned and went back out the door, and Katy sucked in a breath. She would not allow her old, youthful crush to muscle its way in and crowd out her older, smarter self. No way, no how.

She moved toward the kitchen, resolutely passing by the hallway to her bedroom with barely a longing glance. She hadn't planned to do anything more than wash her hands for dinner and refused to give in to her sudden urge to clean up a little and change her clothes. Maybe it would even be a good thing, she thought as she shook her head at herself, if Alec noticed she didn't exactly smell perfume fresh.

"Why didn't you tell me you'd invited Alec for dinner?" she asked Nick in a whisper, even though she hadn't heard the man come back into the house.

"Because he's my best friend, and I didn't realize until tonight that you still felt such animosity toward him." Her brother glanced at her before he turned his attention back to the dinner. "Which I frankly hope you'll get over."

"No animosity. As I told you, I just don't want to be friends with him anymore." And her darned shortness of breath and flippity heart and awareness of his hunkiness quotient was far different from feelings of friendship anyway, dang it. Which made it even more important that they not be together anywhere but at work until her smart brain prevailed over her not-so-smart one. "But obviously, since he's my instructor for the month, I'm perfectly fine with spending work time with him. I just would've appreciated a heads-up."

"Okay. Hey, Katy-Did." Nick turned to her, the evil big-brother smile on his face she was more than used to. "Alec's coming over for dinner."

She rolled her eyes. "Thanks for telling me. If

I'd known it wasn't just the two of us, I wouldn't have dressed up in my nicest clothes."

As Nick chuckled in response, Alec's voice filled the kitchen, followed by his tall, broad form. "You look good in whatever you're wearing, Katy."

She looked up at his eyes that were all golden and warm again, accompanied by a beautiful smile that seemed absurdly sincere, since she knew she couldn't look much more of a wreck if she tried. Why did the darned man have to have the kind of charm that made it all too easy to overlook his not-charming characteristics?

"Thank you." She busied herself with getting the food together, despite both men's protests that she was supposed to be off duty. In short order, they were sitting at the small table, holding crystal glasses and lit, to her touched surprise, with candles.

"To Dr. Katherine Pappas," Nick said, holding up his glass of red wine. "Congratulations on finishing med school with honors and for living through your first day as an intern."

"Cheers to that," Alec said, his focus so entirely on her it was unnerving. "We always knew you were special, and you've proved it over and over again."

Special? And here she'd thought it had been her domain to think of Alec that way when they'd been young. "Thank you. And here's hoping I don't do anything stupid to embarrass you in rounds over the next month."

"You could never do anything to embarrass me, Katy, and that's a fact. I'm more than sure you're going to make me look good."

As if he needed her to make him look good.

They all sipped their drinks, and Katy wasn't sure if it was the wine slipping down her throat that made her chest feel so warm or something else. Something like Alec talking about the faith he had in her, as he had so many times in the past.

Despite it being just the three of them, their meal together brought a welcome feeling of normalcy. Almost like the years hadn't passed and Alec was just hanging out with the Pappas clan for dinner. Except those times would never come again. Her and Nick's father was gone, and

Alec was not the knight in shining armor she'd painted him to be.

"I was called in to help with a rough surgery today," Nick said. "Bob Rollins had a teen girl with a torsion in her ovary, and when he opened her up she was a total mess. Had to bring in another gynecologist and me to dive in there with him to identify and try to save her entire reproductive system. So remember, Katy, don't be surprised if some surgeries turn out to be completely different than you expect." He gave her a pointed look. "Just like people."

It didn't take a genius to know what he was saying. "I'll remember."

Nick turned to Alec. "What time is your flight next weekend?"

"For the wedding? Nine a.m., I think."

"You were able to take time off even though you're doing teaching rounds?" Katy hoped she didn't sound as dismayed as she felt, but she wasn't excited about trying to keep her distance from him at another family event.

"You bet." A grin slowly creased his cheeks.

"Maybe you can help me with my marginal Greek dancing skills."

She stared into his amused eyes then shook her head. Holding his hand in more ways than one? There had been a time when she'd have loved to. "You fake it well, Alec. You don't need anyone's help with that."

CHAPTER THREE

ALEC WONDERED WHY Katy's expression had become strained, just as he still wondered why she seemed so cool toward him. Surely she wasn't still upset about their little kiss from five years ago?

Then there'd be a brief moment when she was more like the old Katy he used to know. He couldn't deny that he wanted to see more of that Katy, who used to think he was great. Why did he miss her former adulation when he was no longer the troubled kid he used to be?

"Are your parents coming to the wedding?" Nick asked.

"I doubt it. They're both still in Russia while Dad teaches how to do his valve-replacement technique there." And he'd be just as glad to not have his father there, grilling him on his life and telling him his surgical work wasn't as important as a cardiologist's.

"I figured you'd have to work," Katy said, "so I hadn't even thought about you coming."

And didn't that make his ego feel great? Though the way she'd been toward him the past times he'd seen her at family get-togethers had shown she no longer thought of him much, period. "Are you really going to make me fake again that I can Greek-dance?" Alec asked, which earned him a small smile from her.

"Nick's the master dancer. He can teach you."

"Never did me much good in the past." It was pretty obvious Katy didn't want to teach him, which gave him a twinge of disappointment. He remembered well the times he'd watched her lead the dancing, mesmerized by her movements and her joyful smile. "What time are you two flying out?"

"Nick has us leaving at some crazy time, like six a.m.," Katy said with a scowl. "As though I'm not already getting zero sleep."

"Think of your lack of sleep as a rite of passage. Kind of like hazing in a fraternity," Nick said with a grin.

"Mr. Empathy, as usual," she said, punching her brother none too gently on the arm. Nick raised both fists, jabbing them in the air back at her.

"Okay, you two." Alec shook his head but at the same time he had to chuckle. Some things never changed. And when it came to the Pappas family, not changing was the best thing in the world, as far as Alec was concerned. "Truthfully, though, the more hours you're in the hospital, Katy, the more you're exposed to all different kinds of cases that are invaluable for learning. The time schedules aren't just for torture."

"I know, I know. I'll try to remember that in the midst of my zombie state tomorrow. I doubt we interns will even be able to stay awake for the after-work welcome dinner with the teaching staff," she said. Her tone might be grumbling, but those blue eyes of hers were lit with the enthusiasm and wonder he'd seen in them, and had always enjoyed, forever. She turned her beautifully lethal gaze on Nick. "Does it sound silly to say I'm really excited to be one of…of you now? A real doctor, like Dad?"

George Pappas. Alec's chest grew a little heavy, thinking of the man who'd been more of a father to him than his own. Knowing how hard it had been on every one of the man's family when he'd died. And on himself too, despite not being a real member of the Pappas tribe.

"Your dad would be proud of you." He reached for her soft hand and squeezed it. "He was proud of each one of you, but I think he had a special place in his heart for his youngest."

Tears filled her eyes, and he kicked himself. The last thing he wanted to do was make her sad. Then she smiled through the tears, and the jab of guilt eased.

"Thank you. I know I don't have much experience yet—that I have a crazy amount to learn. But I think you're right. I think he would be proud that I'm at least trying."

Trying? The Katy Pappas he knew never tried. She worked until she accomplished whatever damned goal she'd set for herself, from the most simple to the most difficult.

"There's no question about that, Katy," Nick said, his voice a little rough. "Here's another toast to you for always making him proud."

"To you, Katy." Alec raised his glass to hers. Maybe it was because she couldn't see too well through the tears in her eyes, but for whatever reason, as she tried to clink her glass to his, she completely missed. And managed to toss most of her glass of wine straight onto his lap.

"Oh! I'm so sorry, Alec!" Katy leaped from her seat, grabbing her napkin to dab vigorously at the wine staining the bottom of his shirt, moving down to dab even harder at the biggest pool of liquid in a place he didn't want her dabbing.

Or maybe he did, because seeing her hands on his groin, feeling them pressing against him, shortened his breath, stepped up the beat of his heart and invited an instant physical response he couldn't control.

"Let me handle it, Katy," he said, firmly grabbing her wrist before she could feel exactly what was happening to him and embarrass them both.

"But the stain is setting, and— Oh!" Suddenly her motions stilled and her widening eyes met his. Obviously, his body's response to her hands all over him was plenty clear.

"Yeah. 'Oh.'" What else could he say? Except maybe, *Touch me some more, please.*

"Katy, having you around sure livens things up." Laughing, Nick headed to the kitchen. "I'll get a wet towel."

"I'm…sorry. Really sorry. So, so sorry." Her face was nearly as red as the wine, and she stood staring at him as though she was frozen.

"It's okay. Really." He should be sorry, too. Sorry that she felt embarrassed, sorry that his clothes might be ruined, and sorry that his body had responded the way it had. In spite of all that, though, he found he didn't feel sorry at all. In fact, his primary feeling at the moment was wishing the two of them were alone so he could strip off his wet clothes and see if that led anywhere good.

As soon as the thought came, the heat that had surged throughout his body was quickly replaced by ice, and he wanted to pummel some sense into himself. Not only was Katy Nick's little sister, she was his student, damn it. He absolutely could not think of her in that way, ever, despite the fact that, right now, he clearly was. But that was not acceptable. Not under any circumstances, but especially while he was her superior at the hospital.

He'd already tried to blow up his own career with that kind of mistake, and had succeeded all too well in blowing up someone else's. The last thing he wanted was to lose the respect he'd tried so hard to regain since his stupidity of the past.

And risking Katy's career and reputation with the same kind of stupidity? Never.

Had she really rubbed her hands all around and pressed down on Alec's privates?

Katy walked down the hospital corridor, face burning as she thought about the reality that, yes, she sure had. Even worse, she now knew something she hadn't before. Which was that he apparently became aroused easily and was more than well endowed.

Long ago, she'd fantasized about—well—all of that. But she knew last night's impressive reaction had had nothing to do with her. Lots of men might respond that way to any woman fondling them, inadvertently or not. And since Alec had gone through girlfriends in high school like a patient with a bad cold went through tissues, she shouldn't be surprised he was one of them.

What was a surprise had been her own reaction. That in addition to feeling beyond embarrassed, she'd also found herself fascinated by the swelling beneath those jeans of his. As though she was some innocent kid and not a grown woman. She was quite sure Alec's swelling—and what a ridiculous way for her, a doctor, to be thinking of his erection—was no more impressive than any other man's. Well, she wasn't sure, but she no longer had any desire to find out. Did. Not.

For the tenth time that morning she shoved down thoughts of any and all of Alec's body parts and headed to her next patient's room. "Good morning, Helen!" Katy stepped to Mrs. Patterson's bedside and patted her thin shoulder. "Ready to go home?"

"I wish I could. But I'm heading back to rehab at the nursing home until I'm stronger."

"I know. But you're going to be out of there before you know it." She took her stethoscope from her neck and pressed the bell to her palm to warm it before she placed it against the woman's chest. "Do you have someone to help take care of you when you're home?"

"My daughter's coming for a bit after I'm home. Today, though, my son is taking me back to rehab."

"That's good." The woman didn't look too excited about that, but who would be? "I know it's not much fun doing rehab, but knowing it's going to make you independent again makes it worth it."

"I don't mind it, really. The nurses and physical therapists are lovely. But all this has been very depressing." Helen sighed. "Until I broke my hip, I was pretty strong and walked my little dogs every day. Now I feel just awful with this stomach pain. It's enough to make me want to move on to heaven to be with my Albert."

The sadness and frustration on the poor woman's face squeezed Katy's heart. She wrapped her arm around Helen's shoulders to give her a hug. "I can imagine how hard it is to feel weak and not well when you're used to being up and about. But your tests don't show any problems, so I bet you're going to be feeling good again soon. Hang in there."

A tall, skinny man with long hair knocked on the doorjamb, which surprised Katy. It couldn't be any later than seven a.m. "Can I come in?"

"Hello, Jeffrey." Helen shifted her gaze from the man to Katy. "Dr. Pappas, this is my son. Jeffrey, this is Dr. Pappas. She's been taking good care of me."

"Thanks for that," Jeffrey said, then came to stand between Katy and his mother, rather rudely. "Mom, I need a little cash to fix my car. Can you front me a loan? I brought your check-book."

"I just gave you money for your car last week." Helen frowned, but took the checkbook he handed her.

"I know, but there's something else wrong now, so I've been driving yours. I'll pay you back soon."

"This has to be the last time. My medical bills

are adding up." Helen scribbled out a check. "Please remember I need you to pick me up whenever I'm released today."

"Okay. Call me." He dropped a quick kiss on her forehead and headed out the door. Katy couldn't believe he hadn't even asked his sweet mother how she was feeling.

She squeezed Mrs. Patterson's hand one more time. "If I don't see you again before you're released, I hope you're back to walking your pups very soon."

Katy left the room and looked at her patient notes. Next was a seven-year-old boy named David, who'd had a complication when his appendix had ruptured. Alec had done the surgery nearly a week before Katy had arrived, but the poor child still had a drain in his belly.

About to knock quietly on David's door in case he was still asleep, she was surprised to hear the deep rumble of a man's voice. Then was even more surprised to see Alec in scrubs, sitting on the side of the boy's bed. What was he doing, seeing a patient so early?

She shoved aside the discomfort that again

heated her cheeks. She had to see the man every day, for heaven's sake, and he'd probably forgotten all about the little fondling incident. "Good morning, Dr. Armstrong. You're an early bird today."

"I wanted to stop in and see our star patient before I start morning surgery." He stood and smiled down at David. "The drain's looking good, buddy. We just might be able to take it out in a day or two."

"I can't wait!" David grinned, showing a missing tooth. "But I'm feeling lots better, Dr. Armstrong. Thanks for the car stuff you brought me. Will you come back and see me later?"

"I'll try, David." He tousled the boy's hair and turned to leave, and his sweet expression and the warmth in his eyes made Katy's breath catch in her throat.

Had she ever seen him around children before? Except back when she'd been a child? She couldn't remember, but it seemed he was pretty good with them. His surgery schedule was so heavy she couldn't imagine he'd be able to come back to see the child later, not to mention that the welcome dinner was tonight, but it was nice of him to tell the boy he'd try.

"I've checked David out, so you don't need to, Dr. Pappas." They moved to the shadow of the doorway where he paused. "What patient are you seeing next?"

They stood so close together she could smell his aftershave, see a tiny spot next to his lips that he'd missed when shaving, feel the heat of his body near hers. Unwittingly, her thoughts turned to touching him the night before, and she started to feel overly warm. From embarrassment, of course.

"Mr. Lyons in 2215."

"Better watch out you don't spill anything on him. Mr. Lyons can be quite a character."

Lord, she'd hoped he wouldn't mention it again. Even in the low light of the room she could see the amused glint in his eyes. His lips tipped up into a slow smile, and she found herself staring at his mouth. Swallowing, she took a step away from him so she could breathe. "Can we please just forget about that? You know I sometimes have a clumsiness problem."

"I'll try to forget about it. But you know what, Dr. Pappas? I'm pretty sure that's not going to happen."

He left the room and she sucked in a breath. Their exchange had smacked dangerously of flirting, and she shouldn't let that happen. Also shouldn't enjoy it, but she'd be lying to herself if she claimed she hadn't.

About to head to her next patient's room, Katy realized she'd been so distracted she hadn't thought to ask Alec to sign Mr. Lyons' release papers. What was wrong with her? Work had to be her number-one focus, dang it.

She hurried down the hall to catch Alec, wishing their last conversation hadn't been about her grabbing his privates. His tall figure stood by an elevator, and she stepped up her pace. "Dr. Armstrong!"

He turned to her, and his gaze swept her slowly from head to toe. Feeling a little breathless from hurrying, she stopped next to him. "I forgot to ask you to sign Mr. Lyons' release papers."

She looked up at him, his eyes meeting hers for a long moment before he reached for the papers. "And I forgot to ask you if you're excited about helping with some surgeries in a few days. I've put you first on the list."

"Is that an honor, or is it because you want me in and out of there before I kill someone?"

"We try not to let interns kill anybody. It's against hospital policy."

So were some other things he hadn't worried about in the past. But, of course, he was joking. "I confess I'm not excited. But I'm sure it will be an interesting experience."

"It will be. Especially for you, Miss Science. Weren't you always the one conducting various weird experiments on the kitchen counter until your mom yelled at you?"

"Is this your way of calling me a geek? I—" Her phone beeped a text message and she looked at it then frowned. This couldn't be right.

"What is it?"

"The nurse says Mrs. Levitz is having a panic attack. Shortness of breath, chest pain, and a fast heartbeat."

"She's the one who had her gall bladder removed by Nick yesterday, right?" Alec asked, his teasing expression instantly replaced by calm professionalism. "Her chart said she's prone to panic attacks. Prescribe lorazepam and see how she does."

Katy frowned up at Alec. "I don't know. I left her only a short time ago and she was fine. Looking forward to being discharged. I just don't see her having a panic attack right now."

"Since she has a history of them, most likely that's what it is. You'll see this more often than you would guess." His eyes were thoughtful, seeming to study her. "But sometimes it's important to listen to your instincts. Go see her. Let Nick know your conclusion and what your thoughts are on what needs to be done."

"Okay. I will. Thanks." She turned and her chest felt suddenly buoyant. How could it not when Alec had basically just told her he had faith in her to figure it out? She had a ridiculous impulse to look over her shoulder to see if he still stood there and was surprised that he was. Not just standing there but holding the elevator door open with his eyes still on her.

Something about his expression made her heart

thump a little, and she realized she was failing miserably in keeping her former crush from rearing its ugly head. Also failing in re-erecting the cool wall she'd been so good at keeping between them before she'd started working there.

"Hello, Mrs. Levitz," she said as she walked into the patient's room. "I hear you're feeling upset."

"I don't know what's wrong." The poor woman was breathing hard and wringing her hands. The brown eyes staring up at Katy were filled with fear. "My chest hurts. I don't feel good. I'm scared."

"Okay, let's take a look," Katy said in a soothing voice as she took her pulse. No doubt about it, Mrs. Levitz was behaving completely differently than she had been only an hour earlier. But why? A panic attack seemed unlikely, despite her chart saying she was prone to them, since she certainly hadn't been worried about going home. Quite the opposite. But something was going on, there was no doubt about that.

"Did something upset or worry you, Mrs. Levitz?"

"No. No. I just started feeling bad all of a sudden."

"Her chart says she often has panic attacks," the nurse said in a low voice as she reset the monitor that had been screeching at the patient's elevated pulse.

"I know," Katy murmured. "But that just doesn't seem right to me, after speaking with her earlier." Think, Katy. What could be going on here that's not obvious? Chest pain, shortness of breath, and elevated heart rate were, indeed, consistent with a panic attack. But as she peered at the monitor next to the bed she noted that Mrs. Levitz's oxygen level was low, too. And a panic attack wouldn't cause that.

With tension rising in her own chest, she pulled out her little medical book and studied it. Thought back to the cases she'd had in med school. Then she nearly shouted *Eureka* as the answer struck her.

Pulmonary embolism. Unusual, but not impossible after gall-bladder surgery, and it would account for every symptom the woman was experiencing. It was a post-op complication she knew every surgeon dreaded. It also had to be diagnosed and addressed immediately.

"I want a CT scan run on Mrs. Levitz," she said to the nurse, adrenaline surging through her. *"Stat."*

CHAPTER FOUR

KATY STOOD IN the park by Mission Bay and breathed in the tangy sea air. This was exactly why she'd wanted to train in San Diego. The beautiful sandy beaches with tall, swaying palms, the emerald-green grass, the deep blue of the water were all utterly breathtaking. Why choose to work in a cold, gray, rainy place when you could be here?

All kinds of people mingled and chatted at this welcome party for students and staff, but she felt like she'd been talking nonstop all day and enjoyed having a little moment of quiet.

A server stopped next to her with a tray of champagne, and she swiped the last of the sand from her hands and took a glass. Hopefully no one had noticed her sneak down to the beach to dig in the sand and see what creatures lived in there. She'd found little gray crabs of all sizes,

and the moment she did she found herself ridiculously looking at the crowd to see if Alec had
arrived so she could show him.

Hadn't she decided to stay cool and as distant
as possible? To keep their relationship strictly
professional as student and teacher?

But the crab discovery had instantly taken her
back to all their adventuring days together. To
how he'd never made fun of her experiments
and discoveries, and in fact had seemed to enjoy
them as much as she had. She'd been shocked
at the disappointment she'd felt when he was
nowhere in sight.

How strange that she still had this ingrained
habit of looking to him now that he was back
in her life, so to speak. She knew it for what it
was, though, which gave her complete power to
control it.

She moved closer to the crowd, figuring she
should socialize a bit and maybe learn something in the process.

"I had so much pizza last night I'm not going
to do justice to the food here," a nurse said to the
group of women she was standing with.

"I know." A different woman chuckled. "Dr. Armstrong bought enough to feed an army, which was really sweet of him. Just because we all worked so late on the emergency perforated ulcer didn't mean he had to spring for dinner for everyone."

"He always does that when we work late. I just love him. If I wasn't married, I'd have his babies."

The group of women laughed and Katy moved on, not wanting to be an eavesdropper. She'd heard women swooning over the hunky surgeon before—but the fact that he bought pizza after a long day? She'd probably want to have his babies too.

No. Wrong thought. All wrong.

As though drawn by some magnetic force, her eyes lifted to the opposite edge of the party, and there stood Alec. Looking even better in casual dress clothes than he did in scrubs—which seemed nearly impossible, since he looked incredible in them—his hair fluttered across his forehead as he spoke with the woman standing next to him.

The woman stepped closer until they were nearly touching. There was nothing professional or distant about their body language as she rested her hand on his biceps, and the woman had a clear, come-hither look on her attractive face. The face of fifth-year resident Elizabeth Stark.

Katy's gut squeezed and her hand tightened on the stem of her glass. Here it was, right in her face. A cold reminder of who exactly Alec Armstrong was in addition to the good-with-children, pizza-bringing surgeon the nurses adored. Why she'd kept her distance from him until working together had made that impossible.

The image bothered her far more than it should have, considering she'd known all about his player reputation of the past, which clearly was also part of his present. Just as she was thrashing herself for feeling illogically disturbed, Alec stepped back from Elizabeth. His lips flat-lined from the cordial smile there a moment ago, and a frown creased his brow.

Then he walked away, leaving Elizabeth staring after him.

Had they had some kind of tiff? Or was it because Alec wasn't like that any more, as Nick had insisted? The thought lightened the weight in her chest. Maybe she'd held onto her disappointment in him for too long. Maybe it was time to let that go, to see the more mature Alec. The man who still had so many of the appealing qualities of his youth.

Surely she was more mature, too. Mature enough to put behind her old crush and hurt at his rejection and accept him as a friend again.

Alec tried not to stare at Katy, making anyone who might notice wonder why, but he couldn't seem to stop his gaze from traveling back to her. The fragrant breeze coming from the bay fluttered the floral dress she wore, which was significantly shorter than her conservative hospital clothes. He knew he damn well shouldn't but he couldn't resist letting his gaze slowly drop from her appealing face down the length of her body. To her breasts, which were completely covered by a neckline that went all the way up to her collarbone but were still all too well outlined by the filmy fabric.

He'd thought, more than once, that no woman looked better in scrubs than Katy. But watching her now, with the wind outlining her body and the evening sun giving her hair a golden glow, he realized she looked even more spectacular outside the hospital.

Smart, sweet, and gorgeous were one damned lethal combination.

When he'd first found out Katy would be coming to Oceancrest as an intern, he'd been pleased, thinking it would be a good chance to renew the friendship she hadn't seemed to want to continue. Never would he have dreamed he'd have so much trouble keeping himself from looking at her every curve, trouble keeping firmly in mind that she was a student and Nick's little sister.

Hell, who was he kidding? After the way he'd responded to her kiss long ago, he should have known. Shouldn't have been surprised at the stirring of attraction he'd felt the second he'd seen her that first day in the coding patient's room. More than a stirring when she'd wiped the wine from his body. Now every time he saw Katy he saw a special woman there was no denying he wanted more than friendship with.

This inconvenient attraction—hell, unacceptable attraction—was a problem he wasn't sure how to deal with.

"Alec." Nick came to stand next to him and he was glad for a reason to stop watching Katy. "You missed the speeches. Which I'm sure you're real sad about."

"Yeah. Not. After hearing the CEO give the same speech at every welcome gathering, I may be forced to write a new one for him myself."

Nick turned his head to the crowd of people mingling in the park then turned back to Alec. "What—or should I say, who—are you looking at?"

"Uh, nobody in particular. Just seeing who's here." Was it that obvious his gaze kept returning to Katy? Of all the many people he didn't want to notice that, number one was Nick.

"I saw one person here who's already singled you out. Elizabeth Stark," Nick said. "Tell me you aren't going to fall for her coming on to you."

"Why would you even ask me that? Since

when are you my father?" Alec frowned at Nick as they walked up the slope of grass. Hadn't he tried his damnedest to make sure he never got involved with any woman at the hospital? To make sure he and his reputation were stainless now? "You know, it was five years ago. At a different hospital. In a different capacity. I think the chief medical officer is the only person here who even knows about it."

"I know that mess is in the past. You're the one who still avoids any woman within a ten-mile radius of the hospital."

"Then why are you on my case about Elizabeth? Who, for the record, I have zero interest in."

"Because Elizabeth is a student, who's made it clear she has more than zero interest in you." Nick stared at him like he'd grown two heads. "Which you sure as hell know is different than just someone working in the hospital."

No one knew that better than Alec. His gaze caught on Katy again, and his stomach twisted. Good to be reminded that he couldn't think of her the way he kept thinking of her. That he couldn't look at her smooth skin and imagine touching it, couldn't think about tangling his fingers in her soft hair, couldn't want to cover her sweetly smiling lips with his own.

Alec gritted his teeth and forced his attention back to Nick as they headed to the food table. "Don't worry. I'll never cross that line again."

Nick nodded, the conversation obviously over, thankfully. "How about that sister of mine?"

Alec's heart nearly stopped. Surely Nick hadn't noticed… Ah, hell. "What about her?"

"She's been saving lives all by herself."

"Saving lives?" The tightness in Alec's chest slid away. "What did she do?"

"You didn't hear?" Nick grinned at him. "One of my patients. Post-op gall bladder, with anxiety disorder. Everybody assumed she just needed a dose of lorazepam to calm her down, but Katy figured out what was really wrong."

Alec remembered Katy talking with him about the patient earlier. "So, what was wrong?"

"I guess Katy just had a gut feeling about it not being a panic attack, despite the woman's history. Ordered a CT scan and found pulmonary emboli. Got her into the ICU, got a heparin drip going and—bam! Alive and well." Nick looked as pleased as if he'd been the one who'd figured out the problem, though, of course, the woman was his patient, too. "Gotta say, I'm pretty proud of her. I don't think too many first-year interns would have thought of that, especially knowing about the patient's anxiety disorder."

"You've got that right." Alec felt a peculiar pride welling up within his chest, which seemed ridiculous. It wasn't as though his teaching had helped her figure it out. And she was Nick's sister, not his. "I've already seen that Katy has good instincts when it comes to patients. Great bedside manner and rapport, too. The only thing she lacks sometimes is self-confidence, so this is bound to give her that." And wasn't that the truth? He couldn't think of anything lacking in the woman, including the sex appeal that just oozed from her without her even being aware of it.

His gaze slipped back to where she'd been and saw she was headed their way. A good chance to congratulate her on her great job with Mrs. Levitz, then mingle with others to keep his distance.

"Hey, Nick! Alec. How can you two stand not to be out here every day? This place is beautiful!" Strands of her silky hair feathered across her face in the breeze, and her slim fingers shoved them aside as she smiled at him.

"It is beautiful. And I'm out here every day I can be. My condo is just across the bay."

"Is it really? I'll bet your view is amazing."

"It is. I could take you sailing or kayaking some time, if you want." Sailing with her sounded great to Alec. Also sounded like a hell of a bad idea, and he quickly changed the subject. "I hear congratulations are in order."

"Congratulations? For what?"

"I know you probably have many things to be congratulated on today." He had to smile at her questioning look. Did she really not know what a great job she'd done? "But I'm referring to figuring out that Mrs. Levitz wasn't having an anxiety attack. Most docs—and especially interns—might not have gotten the diagnosis until it was too late."

"I'm sure that's not true." Pink filled her cheeks, and he realized he loved to see her blush, for some reason. How many women blushed like that these days? "You would have figured it out."

"Probably. Hopefully. But too often we look at the first thing that comes to mind and assume it's the correct thing. With her history of panic attacks, no one could have blamed you for treating her for that and not even considering another possibility. Hell, didn't I tell you to give her lorazepam to see if that did the trick?"

"Yes. But you hadn't seen her as recently as I had."

"I'll bet that in med school you heard about looking for the zebra when everyone else is looking for the horse. That's what you did. You found the zebra no one was looking for, and I'm proud of you. You should be proud of yourself."

"Thank you. I guess I am."

They smiled at one another as the breeze whipped a thick strand of hair onto her face, and he nearly reached to slip it from her eyes and tuck it behind her ear. Nearly leaned forward to kiss her on the cheek. Just her cheek, in celebration, as he would have long ago when they'd been young.

Who was he kidding? He wanted to start on her cheek and work his way over to that smiling mouth.

"I'm proud of you too, Katy," Nick said.

Damn. He'd practically forgotten Nick was there. Alec shifted his attention from the temptation of her lips and noticed she had sand all over her dress.

"You been rolling on the beach?"

"Rolling on the beach?" Her gaze followed his. "Oops. I thought I'd wiped it off. I was digging in the sand to see what was down in there."

He had to chuckle. Typical Katy. "And what did you find?"

"I'm not sure. Can I show you? You might know what they are."

There it was again. That absurd puffing-up-his-chest feeling, as though it meant something that she thought he'd know the answer to a simple question about crustaceans. "You're not pulling a joke on me are you? Have you dug a hole and covered it with palm fronds so I'll fall in?"

"As if I'd spend party time digging a hole big enough to trap you in." She laughed. "You're suspicious because those are the kinds of pranks you and Nick liked to pull."

"Thanks for the reminder. I'll have to think up a good way to prank you for old times' sake," Nick said with a grin. "I'm going to catch up with a few other folks here. You're checking on patients after this, aren't you, Katy? I'll see you when you get home."

"Okay," she said to Nick, but her eyes were on Alec. "Come on. They're down here."

They walked across a long stretch of grass and down a small hill to the water, leaving behind the party guest chatter. He was struck with an absurd desire to wrap his arm around her shoulders or to twine her fingers within his. Maybe it wasn't all that crazy, though—when they'd been young he'd often given her a brotherly hug.

Nothing brotherly about what he was feeling now, though, damn it. What he felt was hot and insistent and getting more and more difficult to tamp down.

"See all these little holes in the wet sand?"

She pointed as the gentle waves receded, leaving bubbly holes behind. "I saw sandpipers and black-bellied plovers poking in their beaks. So I dug down and found some funny-looking gray crabs, some tiny and some as big as a spoon. Do you know what they are?"

"I'm afraid I don't. Folks here just call them sand crabs. And why am I not surprised you know the names of the birds, Miss Science?" Just like when she'd been little, she was curious about everything and because of that had an amazing, encyclopedic brain. He had to smile. That curiosity was going to make her a fine doctor one day.

"Are any bigger than the ones I described?"

"I confess I haven't paid that much attention." He crouched down and she crouched along with him, steadying herself by grasping the back of his arm, her knee bumping against his. They'd explored things this same way long ago, and it felt natural, right, to have her hold on to him that way. "Let's dig up some more to find out."

He scooped into the sand and she scooped and dug along with him, finally pulling out a handful of the grayish crabs in all sizes. "Looks like that's about the biggest one," he said, holding up a fat one. "They do look pretty tasty, don't they? If you're a bird, that is. Sandpipers and... what kind?"

"Black-bellied plovers. Willets, too." She looked up at him and laughed, her blue eyes sparkling. Her face was so close he could feel her breath brush his lips warmly. Teasing him without knowing. Tormenting him. When all he wanted was to press his own lips to her smiling ones.

"I wish I'd brought a bucket to put some in. I'd like to take a few home."

"For what? To keep as pets? Give to the dogs to play with?"

"No, to study, silly." Her teeth flashed white in the wide smile she gave him. "Don't you remember how we'd do that back at home all the time with beetles and locusts and things?"

"I remember." How could he be feeling this sensual pull towards her when they were talking about crabs and beetles and science? Because it was Katy, and that had always been a part of who she was. Because watching her lips move, watching her speak made him think of how he'd felt when she'd kissed him long ago. How it would feel to kiss her now, which was all he wanted to do.

He turned to place the crabs back into the hole they'd dug, to somehow take his mind away from this nearly overwhelming desire to lower her to the sand and kiss her and touch her, and to hell with the consequences.

Their hands touched, her fingers sliding against his as she tucked the crabs into the hole and covered them with sand. About to stand and end the torture of being so close to her, she clapped the wet sand from her hands and lost her balance. Rocked into him, shoulder to shoulder. Crouched on the balls of his feet, Alec wasn't prepared for the impact and promptly fell backward onto his rear, his elbow in the sand holding him half-upright, with Katy falling practically into his lap. One sandy hand slapped against his collarbone, the other grabbed his shoulder.

"Oh! Sorry!" Katy stared down at him, and he thought he saw more in her expression than just apology. He thought he saw a flicker of something in her darkened eyes. Something that was hot and intangible and irresistible and that hung, suspended, between them. Something he'd been feeling all damned day. All damned week.

Without thought, his heart beating fast, Alec wrapped one arm around her. An instinctive movement that brought her against him, her breasts against his chest. Her hair fell in a curtain around her face and tickled his cheeks. He watched her lips part in surprise, breathed in the scent of her that tormented him every time she was near. His sandy hand began to slowly slip up her back to cup her nape, to bring the mouth he'd wanted to kiss all day to his.

The sound of someone laughing poured over his mindless, surging libido like a full bucket of iced water, and he jerked up, nearly tossing Katy into the sand. He stared in horror at her, all too aware of what had just about happened. With a student. With everyone at the hospital just a stone's throw away.

How many times had he vowed to never again make a foolish mistake that could jeopardize his career? Or, damn it, hers, too, which was even more important. He fought for calm in the midst of his self-disgust. "Sorry. I…didn't do a good job of catching you, did I?"

"I'm the one who's sorry. It was my fault. I lost my balance." Her expression was serious, that little frown creasing her brow again, and Alec figured it was probably in reaction to his own expression. He could only imagine what it was. He heaved in a breath, then stood and stretched his sandy hand to hers to help her up. Despite his anger at himself, the feel of her hand within his as he tugged her to her feet still sent that not-allowed zing, which he kept feeling when he touched her, all the way up his arm, and never mind that grit rubbed between their palms, masking her skin's usual softness.

Standing close, she still stared up at him, her blue eyes now wide. Questioning. Did she know how she affected him? She had to, considering she'd been practically lying on him a moment ago.

"Dr. Armstrong I don't think I've had the pleasure of meeting your intern."

Alec swung toward the voice that spoke from directly behind him, and felt like a second, even icier bucket of water had been dumped on his brainless head when he saw who stood there. The only person in the hospital besides Nick who knew about the scandal he'd been involved in long ago. The person responsible for ensuring doctors in the hospital were held to a strict code of ethics.

"Hello, Margaret." He struggled to sound calm and normal. "This is Dr. Katherine Pappas. Katy, meet Oceancrest's Chief Medical Officer, Dr. Margaret Sanders."

CHAPTER FIVE

NEARLY FINISHED WITH checking on patients for the night, Katy stretched her tired muscles and flexed her fingers. Which reminded her of how Alec's grip on her hand earlier, when he'd helped her up from the sand, had become downright vise-like after he'd turned to speak with the CMO. Then how he'd dropped it like it had been a red-hot coal…

And of course she knew why. The woman had likely seen Katy practically sprawled on top of Alec after she'd lost her balance. Might even have seen the way Katy knew she'd been looking at him, which had been with serious thoughts of kissing the man until he couldn't breathe. Alec had probably seen it, too. And since he knew better than anybody the potential consequences of inappropriate conduct between a supervisor and student, he'd practically left divots in the grass after he'd introduced them and taken off.

She smacked the side of her head. Clearly, there was something wrong with her. What kind of woman would kiss a guy again after he'd pushed her away and said he wasn't interested the last time? Only a woman who enjoyed rejection, and apparently she was that woman. A woman who also enjoyed flirting with danger, since that kind of relationship with Alec could jeopardize her own fledgling career anyway.

She looked at her patient list and headed to David's room. Poor little guy had been in the hospital for quite awhile, and she hoped Alec would be able to remove the child's drain soon.

As she approached the room, she heard a man's voice speaking in an almost melodic voice and stopped short of the door. This time she knew who the voice belonged to. Alec.

He'd actually come back to the hospital after the welcome party? After getting here by at least seven a.m. this morning, since that was when she'd seen him in this very room? She may be a newbie, but she'd spent a lot of time in hospitals during medical school and couldn't remember seeing any surgeon do such a thing unless there was an emergency.

He'd told David he'd try to come back, and obviously he'd meant it. Amazed, she couldn't resist peeking inside, even though she knew it was tantamount to spying. Her heart melted into a gooey little puddle at the sight of Alec sitting on the side of the boy's bed, a picture book in his hand with race cars on the front, reading out loud. David stared raptly at the pages, though his eyelids were drooping a bit.

Oh. My. She was supposed to try fighting her attraction to this man? This man who'd always included her in his and Nick's adventures? This man who was now this caring doctor who took the time to keep his word to this child when he could be home with his feet up?

The answer was, yes, she had to, for all the reasons she'd been thinking about just five minutes earlier.

She moved into the room. "Sorry to interrupt. Just wanted to see if you need anything from me."

Alec looked up and his eyes met hers for a

long moment. Something about the expression in his eyes sent her heart thumping harder and made her think of exactly what she needed and wanted from him, even though she shouldn't and couldn't, and how come she seemed unable to keep that firmly in her mind?

"Dr. Pappas. Thanks, but I think David's all set. And ready to sleep, from the looks of it." He stood and pulled the covers up to the child's chin. "Sleep tight, buddy. I'll see you in the morning."

"Night, Dr. Armstrong. Thanks for my book."

Katy followed Alec out the door, where they stood silently. Awkwardly.

"Look, I just have to say I'm sorry I fell on you on the beach." Getting it out there was the best way to clear the air. "I could tell you were embarrassed that Dr. Sanders saw me sort of on top of you."

"I wasn't embarrassed. Don't worry about it." His serious expression said something other than his words, but she wasn't sure exactly what. Concern for her? Guilt?

"Well, anyway. Sorry." She cleared her throat. "I can't believe you came back to see David, and even read him a book. That's a lot more patient care than most surgeons offer."

"I had to come back to see a patient in the ER, so I was here anyway. And most docs would read a book if a kid asked."

"Still, that was really sweet of you."

"Sweet? I'm a lot of things, but sweet isn't one of them."

Oh, yes it was. He was. When he wanted to be. "What about the time I had chicken pox and you smuggled me bubble gum? You stuffed it inside a teddy bear and brought it to me...remember? Or the time I jumped on Nick's skateboard after he told me not to and then fell and skinned up my knees? While he yelled at me, you ran inside and got first-aid stuff."

His face relaxed into a grin. "That wasn't sweet. I just used you as a guinea pig. Was practicing for someday when I became a doctor."

"I hope you've gotten better at it," she teased, glad to replace the awkwardness with their familiar banter. "You put so much ointment on my legs the bandages wouldn't stick. So you wrapped me with gauze and tape until I looked like a mummy."

He laughed. His cheeks, dark with five-o'clock shadow, creased and his eyes twinkled, and despite her prior stern talks to herself, her heart swelled a little in response.

"But you were a very cute mummy." Still smiling, he ran his finger slowly down her nose and her breath grew short at the touch. "I remember—"

Alec's phone rang, and she moved away discreetly to give him some privacy while he answered it. Wondering, since it was so late, if it was a woman he dated. Feeling ridiculously, stupidly jealous at the thought, she wanted to thrash herself all over again.

"We have a blunt trauma cardiac arrest in the ER," he said, moving toward her as he shoved his phone in his pocket. "Stab wound to the chest. I need to do an emergency thoracotomy." He grasped her arm, his hand slipping down to hers as he strode so fast down the hall she had to run beside him. "This is something you'll probably never have a chance to see again."

"Do I have to?" Okay, she knew she sounded like a little kid who didn't want to clean her room. But she wasn't going to be a surgeon, and knew the procedure was only done on someone in an extremely life-threatening situation. Wouldn't she just get in the way?

"Yes, you have to." His intense expression gave way to a quick grin. "I'm your teacher this month and I say so. Believe me, you'll be glad you came along."

He pushed open the stairwell door and released her hand to jog down the steps. "Don't trip," he said over his shoulder. "The stairs are faster than the elevator, and I need to get in there. You can join me when you're scrubbed."

"What, you think I can't keep up with you? You and Nick never succeeded in ditching me in the past."

She could hear his chuckle as he widened the distance between them. "Keep up with me? Sweetheart, you've always been ten steps ahead. See you down there."

Sweetheart? Her breath caught, and it wasn't from hurrying down the stairs. Never, in all the years she'd known him, had he called her that. She shouldn't read anything into it, but the word warmed her heart anyway.

He disappeared through the door to the ER, and she hurried to get ready, nervous but excited, too. An emergency thoracotomy was a rare and difficult procedure, and she knew it was lucky that she'd actually get to see it.

Nothing could have prepared her for the chaos in the OR. It seemed like a dozen people were moving everywhere. Equipment beeped. Tense but controlled voices talked over one another. The patient lay on the gurney as someone steadily performed cardiac compressions on his chest. Alec stood beside a young doctor, who was slicing through the patient's skin from his sternum down between his ribs.

"All the way down to the shoulder, Jason. All the way," Alec said, his voice authoritative but calm. He turned to someone next to him. "We need a bigger knife."

She stood there, taking in the astonishing scene, feeling the sense of urgency in the air, hanging back to stay out of everyone's way. In moments, someone handed another knife to Alec and he stepped close to the patient. "Good job, Jason. I'll take over now. Somebody get the blunt-tipped scissors."

Alec sliced deeper between the ribs, then reached for the scissors and began to cut rapidly, roughly, through the man's flesh and cartilage in a way only a supremely confident and experienced doctor could. Multiple hands reached to hold open the ribs as Alec hacked open the man's body. "Where's the rib spreader? I need it right now."

He lifted his gaze to take the spreader being handed to him, and for a brief moment his intense eyes met hers across the room. He maneuvered the spreader between the ribs and cranked it to widen the opening. And all of it had been done in about one minute.

Part of Katy wished she could see better exactly what was happening, and part of her wasn't sure she wanted to.

"Dr. Pappas, I need you to assist me," Alec said, without looking up.

She gulped and headed to the other side of the

patient, listening to the urgent voices of the nurses and residents as they worked, seeing the ragged flesh around the now wide opening in the man's chest, the blood being suctioned out, the hands still performing steady cardiac compression as Alec finished positioning the spreader.

She felt a little hot and swayed ever so slightly on her feet. Do not faint and take people's attention from this man who might be dying, you fool, she scolded herself as she took a deep breath. She forced herself to move close to Alec. "What do you need me to do, Dr. Armstrong?"

"Hold the clamp in place. I want you to see how I snip then manually spread the pericardium to expose the heart."

Lord, why did he want her to see that? But she knew the answer. Because Alec had shown her so many crazy things over the years, and knew she'd benefit as a doctor to see first-hand how this was done.

Heart pounding, she slid her gloved fingers around the edges of the bloodied spreader and tried to hold it steady as Alec reached into the man's chest cavity.

He made a tiny incision in the pericardium then tugged the membrane apart with his fingers to expose the heart. He then grasped that vital organ in his hand and began to gently massage it. In moments the man's heart was moving, beating, pumping on its own right in front of her eyes, and it was the most amazing thing she'd ever seen.

"Oh, my God!" she exclaimed, looking up at Alec, whose eyebrows were lowered over his supremely focused eyes as he worked. "It worked! He's got cardiac activity!"

Alec nodded. "Somebody get me sutures to repair this small cut in the heart. Mammary artery is bleeding. I need a clamp for that. May have to cross-plant the aorta, too."

The flurry of activity continued as Alec, unbelievably calm, gave orders, repaired the cut in the man's heart, and worked to address the other issues for another hour and a half or so. Katy kept looking at Alec, wondering if he was tiring. Heck, her arms were numb and she was just standing there! But his posture and focused expression never changed.

Finally, it was over. The patient's vital signs were within acceptable range. He was moved to the ICU as everyone beamed, slapped each other on the back and chattered in relief, congratulating each other and Alec.

He stripped off his gloves and yanked down his mask, a broad smile on his face. "Great teamwork, everyone. You all made Oceancrest proud tonight."

"Awesome job, Dr. Armstrong," one of the nurses said. "I'll be honest, I didn't think he was going to make it until you got here."

"I wasn't sure either. But an amazing staff and a little luck made it all work out."

As everyone made their way out of the OR, Alec turned to Katy, his finger moving her hair from her eyes to tuck it behind her ear. "So was I right? Are you glad you were in here to see this?"

She looked at his smile and the crinkles at the corners of his tired eyes. Moved her gaze around the now empty room. Empty except for the blood spattered all over the floor and the instruments and tubing and sponges strewn everywhere, looking like a war zone of sorts. Which it had been. An epic battle to save that man's life.

It was an experience she'd never forget. And the most unforgettable part had been seeing Alec in action under extreme stress.

"Yes. I'm glad I was here."

"You did great. Held the clamp steady and didn't faint on me. I'm proud of you."

"I confess I did feel a little faint for a minute."

"But you controlled it. That's what's important. Besides, Miss Science wouldn't want to miss one of the coolest surgeries there is."

His eyes, full of admiration, met hers, and she could picture the little pit-pat her heart was doing in her own chest since she'd just seen, incredibly, that man's heart pumping inside his.

Alec may have made a big mistake in the past, but she could no longer deny that today he was pretty much the total package. Uber-talented. Generous and appreciative of his staff. Beyond caring for his patients.

"Thank you for including me." As he always had. "It was an incredible experience."

"We make a good team." He moved closer,

cupped her face in his palms, his eyes focused as intently on her now as they'd been on his work.

To her shock, his mouth lowered to hers in a light touch, at first soft and warm, then firmer, hotter, and she found herself wrapping her arms around his neck, sinking into the incredible, delicious sensation of kissing him. Of him kissing her.

Her heart beat hard and her breath grew short, and just as she was about to open her mouth in invitation to a deeper exploration, he pulled away. His eyes now the darkest she'd ever seen them, his chest rose and fell in a deep breath.

"Congratulations on getting through it like the superstar you are," he said, his voice rough. "Tomorrow's rounds won't be as exciting as tonight's surgery but I promise to make it as good as it can be."

Staring after him as he walked out the door, she lifted her fingers slowly to her lips, wondering why he'd kissed her. And thinking about what she'd really like for him to make as good as it could be.

CHAPTER SIX

CONSIDERING HER LACK of sleep all week, it was hard to believe anything could have kept Katy awake. But she'd found herself wound up after the exhilaration of watching Alec perform that amazing surgery. Not to mention the feel of his lips had still been imprinted on hers, questions swirling through her mind. She hadn't gotten to sleep until the wee hours of the night, and by the following afternoon even constant hits of coffee couldn't keep her from dragging.

She tried to come up with how many hours she'd slept the past couple of days, but finally decided it didn't matter. All she knew was that she was so tired her vision was starting to blur.

About to check on another patient on the floor, her call system buzzed.

"Dr. Pappas."

"Becky from ER here. We have a fifteen-year-old girl with abdominal pain and want Surgery to check her out, rule out any surgical necessity, and sign off on her."

As she headed to the ER, she realized her hands weren't sweaty and she knew exactly what to do when she got there. Interview the patient, give her a physical exam, order blood work then check the results. She'd come pretty far the past week, and the thought managed to perk her up a bit.

A resident was stepping out of the patient's room when Katy got there. "Anything I should know before I talk with her?"

He shrugged and shook his head. "Tenderness in the belly, but it seems unremarkable. I ordered blood work, CBC and urinalysis. Should be able to look at results soon."

"Okay. Good." A young teen lay on the gurney and a well-groomed woman sat in a chair next to her. "Hi, I'm Dr. Pappas. You must be Emma." She smiled at the girl then turned to the woman. "Are you a relative?"

"I'm Emma's mother. Barbara Brooks."

"It's nice to meet you both." Thank heavens

the girl didn't look like she was in acute pain or at death's door. "I hear you're having some tummy pain. Want to tell me about it?"

"It just...hurts kind of right here." Emma pointed to her belly button.

"Okay, let me see." She snapped on gloves and gave her a general physical exam, noting no pain in the right or left quadrants. Probably not gall bladder or appendicitis. "Have you had any vomiting? Does it hurt when you go to the bathroom?"

"No. I did throw up a few times, but just in the morning."

"All right." She glanced at the mother and then back at Emma. "Do you have a boyfriend? Are you sexually active?"

"No! I don't have a boyfriend."

Barbara nodded in agreement. "No boyfriend so far, I'm happy to say. She's too young for that."

"Okay." She studied the girl's face and couldn't tell if she was fibbing or not. "Mrs. Brooks, would you mind if I speak to Emma alone?"

The woman bristled visibly. "I most certainly

do mind. She needs me here to support her, and I want to hear everything that's discussed."

Katy inclined her head, wondering how she'd get a chance to talk to Emma privately. For now, she'd check the girl's blood work and see if the ER resident had ordered a pregnancy test. "I'm going to check what your blood work shows, but try not to worry." She patted the girl's arm and smiled at her, hoping to soothe the worried look from her brown eyes. "I bet this is just some tummy bug that's got hold of you. Back in a minute."

Katy dodged the nurses and techs, as well as the EMTs that were wheeling in new patients they'd brought in by ambulance, as she made her way to the computers.

"Dr. Pappas?" The ER resident stopped her in the hallway. "I need you to see another patient, Samuel Green in Room 26, and evaluate for surgery. Possible bowel obstruction. Evaluate and report back to me."

"I'll see him as soon as I check the test results for the patient with abdominal pain and I get my report to you about that." Whew! The ER was a crazy place, and she felt glad again that she'd decided to go into family practice medicine, where she could take time to get to know her patients.

Emma's blood work and urinalysis were normal, with no sign of infection, so Katy felt satisfied to report that she didn't have any condition requiring surgery. No pregnancy test on file, though.

She found the busy ER resident and reported her findings. "She's clear to have the medical intern take a look at her now, except for one thing."

He didn't look up from the computer files. "What?"

"There wasn't a pregnancy test ordered. Do you want me to order it?"

He shook his head and headed down the hall, speaking over his shoulder. "I'll have the medical intern do it."

She nodded and moved to see the next patient, studying the papers in her hand, when her head ran smack into Alec Armstrong's hard sternum as he strode down the emergency department corridor.

"Oh!" She stared up at Alec as his hands

grasped her arms to steady her. He shook his head, and her gaze got stuck on the curve of his lips, which sent her breathing a little haywire as she thought of the way he'd kissed her last night. "I'm so sorry. I should have been watching where I was going."

"Walking in a busy hospital while staring downward is asking for trouble," he said, a touch of amusement in his voice. His hands still held her arms, warm and steady, even though she was no longer in danger of toppling over, which seemed to be a common problem when she was around him. As was her heart rate zooming and her mouth going a little dry.

"I know. I guess I can't chew gum and talk at the same time."

"There's no gum chewing allowed in the hospital." He grinned and released one of her arms, holding out his palm. "Spit it out before I have to give you detention."

"What, now you're Mrs. Smith from Highland High School?"

"She probably never gave perfect Miss Katy Pappas detention, but she slapped Nick and me with plenty." He leaned closer, his eyes mischievous, his voice low. "Maybe I should keep you after class to sharpen my pencils."

"Sharpen your pencils? That would be a cakewalk compared to being in charge of washing every test tube and Petri dish, like you and Nick always had me do. Which never occurred to me was completely unfair."

He laughed. "You were so much better at it than we were, you probably would have done them over again anyway." A nurse headed their way, and Alec dropped his hand from her arm. "I was called down here to talk about the teen patient you saw. Did you—?"

"Dr. Armstrong." A nurse stepped up to them, standing close. She glanced over her shoulder then looked back at Alec again. "I know Dr. Platt called you down because your intern didn't order a pregnancy test for the patient." She leaned closer to Alec, waving a piece of paper and giving him a conspiratorial smile. "Just wanted you to know I got it ordered. And also wanted you to know that Dr. Platt didn't spend more than one minute with the girl and left the history and physical completely to surgery. So if he gives you grief about it, you have some ammo to throw back."

"Thanks, Ruth." Alec smiled and, to Katy's astonishment, gave the woman a little wink. "What would I do if you didn't have my back down here?"

Ruth beamed. "What would we do if we didn't have you to deal with some of the other docs around here?" She handed him the paper and winked back. "Good luck."

He looked at the paper and his lips twisted before he turned to Katy. "Okay, teaching moment here. Whenever—"

"Well, it looks like our little helpers don't know what the hell they're doing, doesn't it, Dr. Armstrong?" A short man whose name tag said Dr. Edward Platt strode up to them, with the ER resident Katy had talked to walking behind him. The younger man's expression bore a strong resemblance to a dog who had his tail firmly tucked between his legs. "Both my resident and your intern apparently don't know that any adolescent female who walks through these doors is assumed to be pregnant until we know otherwise."

"I was just about to discuss the case with Dr. Pappas," Alec said in a surprisingly cool voice. Cooler than Katy could remember ever hearing him speak.

"So let's discuss it together," Dr. Platt said with a smirk that hovered between nasty and self-satisfied. "Why didn't you order a pregnancy test, Dr. Pappas? Do you have any idea the liability to this hospital, and to me personally, if we ran radiological tests on a pregnant woman because we were too lazy and careless to check?"

"I..." Katy swallowed, hands sweating, heart pounding, completely taken aback at the hostility on the man's face. She glanced at the resident. Should she say he'd told her he'd take care of ordering the test? "I asked the patient if she was sexually active, and she said no. However, I did—"

"Well, it's another miracle of immaculate conception." He threw up his hands and the condescending expression on his face made Katy literally quake in her shoes. "Was her mother in the room? Did you shoo her out before you asked? Anybody with half a brain knows a teen-ager isn't going to tell the truth about something like that when Mommy or Daddy are around."

"Actually, Dr. Platt, I am aware that—"

Alec took a step forward so that he was in front of Katy, and she had an urge to slip all the way behind him to hide. She made herself stay put, but was grateful for the slight protection and distance from the man throwing figurative darts at her. "It's certainly true that not order-ing the test is a serious mistake. A mistake both these doctors will make only once in their ca-reers, and that day seems to be today. Luckily, we have great staff who ordered the test before anyone else even saw the girl."

"What if we aren't so lucky next time? I don't want a lawsuit on my hands or my ass raked over the coals because of these two being inept."

"Dr. Pappas is far from inept. She is excellent with patients and did a stellar job assisting me just last night in an emergency surgery." Alec's cool tone had grown harder, flintier, as had his eyes. Those tiger eyes, defending Katy as he'd done so many times in her life. "Maybe this wouldn't have happened if you'd done any kind of history and physical on the girl yourself. If you'd spent any time with the patient before either of them did."

"That's why we have the residents and interns." Dr. Platt's face flushed as his eyes narrowed at Alec. "That's their job."

"Well, that's where you and I differ. I think it's my job." He met the man's gaze, his expression steely. "The residents are my backup, not the other way around. Now, if you'll excuse me, I'd like to speak with my intern about this alone."

Alec turned and walked away. Katy followed, immensely glad to get away from the angry Dr. Platt. Alec may be upset with her, too, but she knew he wouldn't flay her skin from her body and leave her bleeding, figuratively speaking.

Silently, she followed him down the corridor and through to another longer, empty corridor. She started to wonder if maybe they were going somewhere private enough that he could flay her after all. Or spank her, she thought, nearly laughing nervously as she thought of his earlier teasing. Except there wasn't anything funny about her messing up with the test.

He finally stopped short of the swinging double doors that led to Radiology and turned to her, his expression thoughtful. But not annoyed or disappointed, thank heavens.

"All right, Katy-Did. Fess up. What happened with the test?"

She inhaled a breath, glad it was Alec she was ratting the ER resident out to. But it didn't make her blameless. "I asked the resident if he wanted me to do it, but he said he'd handle it. I'm sorry, I realize I should have done it anyway. That was a mistake."

Her extreme lack of sleep must be making her embarrassingly overemotional, because just seconds ago she'd wanted to laugh and now, out of the blue, a lump formed in her throat, and to her horror tears stung her eyes.

Since when was she a wimpy, teary girl of an intern just because she'd made an error and someone had yelled at her? She wanted to be strong and tough and capable and the awful awareness that she was none of those things at that moment sent the tears spilling over. Quickly, she turned away, swiping her fingers against her cheeks. No way could she let herself be all weepy and weak like this.

She squared her shoulders and took a deep breath. "I'm…I'm sorry."

He grasped her arms and turned her toward him. His gaze had softened and his hands moved up to cup her face. His thumbs feathered across her cheeks, wiping away her tears with a gentle touch. "Hey, what's all this?"

"I just…feel stupid. I hate making mistakes." As she struggled to control her frustration with herself, she found herself staring at the fine lines at the corners of his eyes, at the thickness of his lashes, just before he gathered her into his arms and folded her against his chest.

His embrace was beyond comforting. His chest, wide and warm and firm, was the absolutely perfect place to lay her tired head. The sound and feel of his steady heartbeat against her cheek, the arms holding her close, and the heady scent of him in her nose had her wrapping her own arms around his back without even considering that she shouldn't.

"Hate to break it to you, but you're human, Katherine Pappas. And humans make mistakes. As for being stupid? Now, that's about the only thing I've ever heard you say that is stupid." His voice rumbled through her, warm and amused, as his wide palm held her cheek to his heart and his lips grazed the top of her forehead. "Being an intern is tough. There's a lot to learn and you thought someone else was going to do it. Now you know it's better to just take care of those details yourself. Remember this is a teaching hospital, and my job is to teach you. Every day that you're working, I'm here to help. I'm here in whatever way you need me to be."

Any way she needed him to be? She lifted her head and looked into his eyes, no longer the flinty tiger eye they'd been in the ER but now golden amber, looking at her with an expression she couldn't quite interpret. An expression that felt more than just comforting. And as she stared into them, she imagined that a hot flicker touched his gaze. His chest rose and fell against hers as his arms tightened around her.

"Thank you," she whispered, her breath short, oh, so aware of how closely they held one another. How good it felt. "I'm sorry to be a crybaby. I'm just really tired, that's all."

"You, a crybaby?" He pressed his smiling lips to one damp cheek, lingered, then kissed the other. "You were the toughest little girl in the world, and now you're one tough intern. Who dove into a thoracotomy without blinking an eye?"

With his breath feathering across her face, her lips, an overwhelming urge to lift up onto her toes and press her mouth to his was nearly impossible to ignore. Thinking about that, and how amazing it had felt last night, sent her back to all the years she'd dreamed of kissing him when she had been a teenager and he a young man.

And to the moment five years ago when she'd kissed him and he'd quickly given her the brush-off, saying anything but friendship between them would be all wrong.

It would be even less right today.

The memory of that humiliating moment had her lowering her arms and she began to step back at the same moment his face lowered an inch and his lips touched hers.

Her eyes slid closed as she savored the sweet sensation. Had he kissed her last night in congratulation? Was he kissing her now in comfort? As his mouth moved slowly, gently, on hers, she didn't care why. She just wanted to feel.

The radiology doors swung open and Alec's head snapped up before his arms dropped and he quickly stepped back. As someone wheeled a gurney into the hallway, a gust of air through the doorway cooled all the warmth she'd felt just a moment ago.

"I'll stop back into the ER after you work up your next patient," he said in a stiff, professional tone. "Sounds to me like he will be a surgical candidate, but we'll confirm that after you run some tests." Abruptly, he turned and strode back down the long hall.

Katy watched him. Couldn't help but notice how his wide shoulders filled out his green scrubs, his tight butt in those loose pants still somehow so unbelievably sexy she couldn't stop looking at it. Then wanted to smack herself.

Her focus had to be on becoming the best doctor she could be. The kind of doctor her father had been—confident, kind, respected and admired. She couldn't allow anything, even delicious Alec Armstrong, to interfere with that goal.

"That would be great, Barney. Thanks. I owe you." Alec turned off his cell, sucked in a breath of relief, and strode down the hospital corridor to check a patient's chart as tension eased from his chest.

Unbelievable that, after all he'd been through five years ago, he'd nearly been caught holding his student intern close against him, murmuring words in her ear and kissing her. Right there in the hallway outside Radiology.

How could he have let himself kiss her in the OR last night? Was he out of his mind? Apparently the answer was a resounding yes.

Something about Katy simply reached inside him. Something that made him want to be there for her, comfort her when she was distressed and not believing in herself. Something that made him forget their student–teacher relationship, forget that she was his best friend and partner's little sister, forget she was completely off-limits for any kind of relationship other than those that came with a little distance.

He'd fought those feelings for the past week, and definitely wasn't doing a good job of it. He'd been so pumped after the successful thoracotomy, so impressed with the way Katy had hung in there, he'd found himself kissing her before he'd known he was going to. And when her beautiful eyes had filled with tears, he'd had only one thought in his head, which had been to hold her close. Once she'd been in his arms, kissing her again had seemed like the most natural thing in the world.

The final realization that he was in serious trouble had come when, as he'd been comforting Katy, he'd spied a roomful of empty gurneys and could think of only one thing. Which had been sweeping up his intern to lie down on one of those beds with him on top of her, making love together until she'd forgotten everything but the feel of him buried inside her.

Damn it. What the hell was wrong with him? Before tongues began to wag, before anything bad could happen to her reputation and career, he realized he had to take himself off the teaching service for the rest of the month. Not an easy thing to accomplish, since every one of the general surgeons had crazy schedules.

Barney Boswell, though, had been willing to switch. Take over for him now, and having Alec do teaching rounds in August. Barney had actually been happy to, since he had a second kid heading to college and wanted to be involved in helping her move in, which would require taking a few extra days off.

So now all Alec had to do was come up with some excuse for why he'd switched with Barney, something convincing and not suspicious. Get through tomorrow, when he and Katy were scheduled to go to the free clinic together. Then after that somehow steer as clear as humanly possible from Katy Pappas.

"How's Katy doing, Alec?"

He looked up to see Nick had just walked out of a patient's room. Apparently not talking about Katy was going to be nearly as challenging as not thinking about her. But he couldn't mind giving her the praise she deserved.

"She's incredible. Did she tell you about the emergency thoracotomy? For a woman who's going into family practice, she was tough as nails through the whole thing."

"I can't believe you got her to go in with you. Good for her. I hear she's good with patients, too."

"She is. Unlike you, who has such a lousy bedside manner you probably should have been an anesthesiologist instead of a surgeon. Though at least your patients are asleep half the time you're around them."

Nick chuckled, probably because this was something he'd been razzed about more than once, not only from Alec but other hospital workers. His ex, too, and Alec wondered if his lack of empathy about her problems had contributed to their marital difficulties.

"Yeah, yeah. Having a touchy-feely bedside

manner isn't as important to my patients as my excellent surgical skills. Which even you, Dr. Golden Hands, must acknowledge I have." He grinned. "I really just wanted to ask if there was anything I could do to help her."

"Starting tomorrow, you'll have to ask Barney, because he's taking over teaching rounds this month."

"You're kidding. Why?"

"He wanted off next month's rounds so he could move his daughter into her college dorm. So we switched." Which was true, except it had been Alec who'd initiated it.

Nick frowned. "Barney's a good guy, but you're a better teacher. I'd hoped—"

"Hello, Doctors. Doing anything fun after work?" Alec's fifth-year resident, Elizabeth, stepped over to put away a chart, smiling at Alec the way she often did, and it was a smile that made him feel distinctly uncomfortable. It was the smile of a woman trying to use her sex appeal to ingratiate herself with her superior.

While it didn't happen often, it did happen occasionally. Alec knew it was tough going for a woman wanting to be a surgeon, and it wasn't unusual for them to feel like they had to work harder to get respect. To be either hard-nosed and aggressive or use their feminine wiles to get ahead. He wished Elizabeth wasn't one of them, and he also wished he could just come out and tell her the way she was coming across. But that would open a can of worms he absolutely did not want to open.

"We have a couple of tough cases this afternoon, Elizabeth," Alec said, keeping the conversation on work. "Are you ready?"

"I'm always ready." The smile she gave made the double entendre more than obvious.

"Dr. Stark," Nick said, his tone and eyes cold, "Dr. Armstrong and I were having a private conversation, if you don't mind."

"Oh. Sorry." She looked both disconcerted and annoyed. "I'll see you in surgery later, Alec, er, Dr. Armstrong."

When she was out of hearing range Nick looked around before speaking. "That woman is getting more obvious every day with her come-ons to you. You need to talk to her about it. The last thing you need is rumors about you and a student to start up. It could dredge up your past and jeopardize your job."

Wasn't that the truth? The thought sent a cold chill running down his spine. He'd worked too hard to earn the respect of his peers. To put behind the lack of respect he'd unfortunately managed to earn five years ago.

The rumors he was worried most about had to do with his attraction to Nick's sister. And the thought of damaging her reputation was a hell of a lot worse than any thoughts of damaging his own. "Don't worry. I steer as clear of Elizabeth as possible. On the occasions I'm at the Flat-Foot Tavern and she shows up for a drink, I leave as soon as I can."

He knew it would take a Herculean effort to stay strictly professional with Katy tomorrow at the clinic, but he had to do it. And if Katy showed up at the bar for after hours "liver rounds," he'd have to somehow make sure he treated her just like any other member of the gang.

CHAPTER SEVEN

KATY TRIED TO keep her eyes on the road and thoughts on what she might learn at the free clinic, but found her gaze drifting more than once to Alec. To his attractive profile and the broadness of his shoulders in a dress shirt and tie instead of his usual scrubs. He swung his car into the lot of a strip mall and parked the car. Katy turned to him in surprise.

"This is where the free clinic is?"

"Yep. It's central to a lot of low-income neighborhoods, and easy to access by bus, too," Alec said. "You already know we have a sizable indigent population here also, and this location serves them well."

He led the way into the clinic, which had a modest but tidy waiting room, and through to a common room, with doors to exam rooms. "This is where the nurses take patients' vital signs, weigh them, and get general histories," Alec said, as he put down his bag then picked up some charts. "There are four exam rooms off it."

"What do you usually do here?" she asked, as she looked around the small space.

"Various stuff. Hernia repair, skin biopsies, chronic wound care, things like that."

"How often do you come? Do all the doctors at Oceancrest work here sometimes?"

"No. It's on a volunteer basis. Nick and I come about once a month. We both think it's important to give to the community, and plenty of other docs do too, but not all of them."

Having already met a lot of doctors at the hospital, she could guess which ones might not. Then again, that would make her judgmental, and she knew from experience you couldn't always judge a book by its cover.

Alec being the most difficult book of all to read.

One minute he was the teasing Alec she used to know, then the new Alec who looked at her the way she used to dream he would. A new Alec who had kissed her twice now, and while she couldn't deny she had enjoyed it she wasn't sure exactly how it made her feel. Well, other than turned on, that was.

He'd turned her down flat five years ago when she'd kissed him. So could his kissing her now be all about the conquest and nothing more? Or was she reading something into it that wasn't there at all? That it really had been just his way of congratulating or comforting her? No matter what it was, Katy scolded herself, she had to stop wondering. While years ago a relationship between them wouldn't have been off-limits, as he'd stated at the time, now it most definitely was.

"Since you're going into family practice, why don't you see Miss Kraft first? She's twenty-four years old with possible cellulitis of the arm. She's already had her vitals taken and is waiting in room two," Alec said, as he looked at the chart, all business. Which was good. "I'm going to do a follow-up with a patient who is post-gallbladder removal. Shouldn't take me long, then I'll join you."

"All right." She took the chart and knocked on the door of the exam room before going in.

A young, attractive woman sat there in a

sleeveless dress, and even from across the room the redness of her arm was obvious. Katy introduced herself then sat next to her. "Can I take a look at your arm? Tell me what happened."

"It's been real red and hurting for a few weeks now. I went to the ER at Oceancrest and they prescribed me antibiotics, but they haven't helped."

Katy gave her a physical exam, and the woman's arm was hot to the touch. The redness ran from her forearm all the way up to her biceps. "Did you fall down? Did you have some kind of skin injury?"

"No. I don't think so. I don't know how it got like this."

Katy looked at her arm a few more minutes, asked a couple more questions, then decided to look at the records from the hospital. Excusing herself, she went into the hallway to the computer and saw that it was her nemesis, Dr. Platt, who'd seen the woman. The antibiotic he'd prescribed was clearly not the right one, and Katy couldn't help but feel a little smug.

Alec came out of the exam room he'd been in and stood next to her, looking at the computer screen along with her. "What do you think, Dr. Pappas?"

"Patient has cellulitis, and our Dr. Platt prescribed cephalexin. It seems clear it's MRSA and that she needs tetracycline."

"Slow down there, Katy-Did." His eyes crinkled at the corners. "How do you think she got the MRSA? Did she fall? Have a pimple that got infected?"

"She says she didn't fall, and doesn't know why she has it."

"Okay, then, Miss Science. What did I say on your very first day? Why do you think she has it? It has to have come from something."

Katy stared up into his smiling eyes and heard loud and clear what he was saying. What he was teaching her. That she'd taken the cellulitis diagnosis at face value, had been pleased with herself, thinking she was smarter than Platt, and hadn't looked any further for a real diagnosis.

"I hate it when you're right," she said, and warmed at the grin he gave her in response. "I wasn't careful enough getting the patient's history. I don't yet have a real diagnosis, do I?"

"Bingo." His hand reached to cup her cheek, his thumb briefly stroking before he dropped it. "You're close to your gold star for the day, Dr. Pappas. Let's go talk to her together."

Alec sat on the stool next to the patient. Katy found herself studying the way he smiled at the woman, reassuring and warm. He asked a few questions and examined her infected arm then the other, though she resisted briefly. Looking more closely now, she could see a few tiny track marks on the skin of both arms, and shook her head at herself. How could she have missed them? Because she hadn't looked carefully enough, but she would never make that same mistake again.

"I hope you know that all we want is to help you, Miss Kraft. And we can't do that unless we're honest with one another. Can we be honest here?" The sincerity in his eyes as he spoke squeezed Katy's chest. Never could she remember hearing a surgeon speak with such understanding to a patient with addiction. With such compassion.

The patient stared at him a moment before her face crumpled and she began to cry. Katy reached for her hand, her own throat closing. "I don't know how it started," the woman said, sobbing. "I just thought it would be a one-time thing. My old boyfriend asked me to give it a try. But then I started shooting up more. And now I don't know how to stop."

"All right. I want you to know you're not alone in this." He reached to squeeze her shoulder. "Dr. Pappas and I are going to get your arm fixed up. I can feel a clot in your vein that's causing the infection and needs to be taken out. After that, there are people here who can help you with your addiction. Okay?"

"Okay." The patient sniffed and wiped her eyes with the tissue Katy handed her. "Thank you. Thank you for helping me."

Katy watched Alec give the woman a local anesthetic then make an incision in her arm to access the vein and remove the infected clot. Her attention kept going from his talented hands to his face as he worked. His dark lashes fanning his cheekbones, his lips pressing together, his eyebrows twitching as he cut and stitched.

Her heart stuttered as she watched him. What a

beautiful man. How could she ever have thought he was beautiful on only the outside and not the inside too?

After tying off the vein, he showed her how to drain off the surrounding pus, then wrapped the wound and prescribed tetracycline. Once they were finished, he spoke to the nurse and social worker who took over.

"You were wonderful with her, Alec." Katy looked up at him and wanted to cup his cheek with her hand, as he'd done to her. Wanted to wrap her arms around him to show him how much she admired what he'd done. Who he was.

"So were you. I'm glad you were here today. This is the kind of patient you might get in your practice. To look at her, you wouldn't guess she's a heroin addict. But there are more functional addicts out there than you would ever guess."

"I'm glad, too. Especially since you schooled me."

He laughed. "Schooled you? That sounds kind of negative."

"Not negative at all. You taught me again to not assume the correct diagnosis is the first thing that comes to mind. To look beyond that for a cause. I knew it, but promptly forgot it when it seemed obvious. You reminded me about looking for the zebra instead of the horse."

He touched his finger to her brow and tapped a few times before tracing it slowly down her nose. "If you can remember that, and I know you will, Dr. Pappas, you're going to be the best doctor at Oceancrest."

She lifted her hand to grasp his. Stared into his warm, smiling eyes, lowered her gaze to the curve of his lips, and knew she was right back to where she'd been all those years ago when she'd written about him in her journal. To when she'd kissed him at her brother's wedding.

But this time it was different. She was different. She was older and wiser and she no longer saw him through the filter of rose-colored glasses. Now she saw him for who he was. A man who was flawed like anyone else, who was capable of making mistakes. A man who was smart and funny and beyond talented, and who cared deeply enough about others to volunteer at a free clinic and take care of anyone who needed his understanding expertise.

A man she so wanted to know more deeply and intimately. Could there be any possibility of that happening, without risking her career in the process?

CHAPTER EIGHT

ALEC STOOD AT the edge of the crowded ball-room, watching the bride and groom dance their first dance together as husband and wife, their big extended family smiling and clapping.

Funny how being around the entire Pappas clan just felt right. The years he'd spent at their house, having lively conversations and disagreements over dinners, intervening in various sibling squabbles, going on day trips crammed into their van, had been some of his happiest childhood memories.

Even now, he felt the tiniest pang that he was, in truth, an outsider, looking in. Still wished, as his childhood self had, that his own family was as close and caring as the Pappas family. That he had a real brother or sister to argue with and be close to. A parent that respected him, believed in him.

The meal had been served, the cake cut, and traditional Greek pastries filled a long table. Earlier, as Elena Pappas had walked down the aisle of the Greek Orthodox church, on Nick's arm, he'd known everyone acutely felt the absence of the bride's father and were doubtless feeling it again at that moment. The wise and gentle man whose dry sense of humor had often found just the right quip to bring strife in the house to a halt and bring on laughter instead.

He thought of how cool Katy had been to him at the past two family weddings. Even at her father's funeral. It had bothered him. A lot. He'd wished he could go back in time and react to Katy's kiss differently. How, exactly, he wasn't sure, since it had shocked the hell out of him as much as his own reaction had. But at least their friendship seemed back on track.

Friendship? Back on track? The smoldering attraction he felt for her now was nothing like friendship and a whole lot like admiration and desire.

She'd constantly impressed him all week. Then working with her at the clinic, she'd made a typical young doctor mistake. But instead of bashing herself about it, or making excuses, she'd quickly realized her error, backtracked, and listened, which too many students didn't do. When she'd looked up at him, telling him how great he was, he'd realized no one had ever made him feel the way she did. Appreciated and admired, and he'd wanted her to know he felt the same way about her. Had nearly gathered her up in his arms for another kiss, but had forced himself to keep his hands off.

His eyes had been on Katy through the whole wedding. The woman was attractive as hell in anything she wore, including scrubs. But today she looked like an angel from heaven, though as soon as the thought came, he rolled his eyes at himself. How corny could he be? Yet that was exactly what she made him think of.

The bridesmaids wore dresses that were a dark purple and strapless, showing off the smoothness of Katy's shoulders and the golden skin above her breasts where a strand of pearls lay. Her thick hair was piled on her head, with wispy tendrils around her face and down her neck, and the sapphire of her eyes was as intensely blue as the stained-glass windows of the church had been.

As she'd followed the newlywed couple back down the aisle, her gaze had caught his, and her smile had somehow ratcheted even higher, seeming to reach right into his chest to squeeze his heart. To reach out and grab him by the throat. And he was damned if, as he'd watched her disappear through the doors, he hadn't thought of someday when she had her own wedding, and of how incredibly beautiful she would look. He felt a deep stab of envy for whoever the lucky guy would be. Knew that might be the first Pappas wedding he wouldn't attend.

He brought his thoughts back to the present and noticed that Katy had moved onto the dance floor with a groomsman. All he wanted to do was watch her, look at her. Ask her to dance with him next. Which was not a good idea, even outside the hospital. He had to find ways to keep his distance, not look for excuses to hold her close.

He forced himself to look away from Katy and glance around the ballroom to see who he might know. A number of attractive women stood in groups, laughing and smiling and openly flirting with the men standing with them. At any other wedding reception Alec might have been interested in meeting some of them. Maybe even enjoy a brief fling for a night or the weekend. But as he turned back to watch Katy dancing, as the music drew to a close and another man approached her, he knew he wouldn't find one other woman he'd rather spend time with than her.

He turned away, no longer wanting to see her in someone else's arms.

A soft hand closed loosely around his wrist, and his heart gave a little stutter when he saw Katy's sweet face smiling up at him.

"I haven't had a chance to talk to you all day," she said. "Wasn't it a beautiful wedding?"

"Beautiful." And watching her had been the most beautiful part of it, her every emotion sending shadows and joy across her face as she'd stood at the front of the church.

"I love Elena's dress. Though I guess men don't care about things like that."

Not unless the dress was wrapped around a smart, gorgeous, adorable woman. Then unwrapped off her. "Your dress is nice too. In fact, you look…very nice." And wasn't that a clumsy comment? But he couldn't tell her what he was really thinking and feeling.

"Thank you." Her smile seemed genuinely pleased, as though it had been a great compliment instead of the lame one he knew it was. It was just like Katy. A woman who was always herself and didn't fish for compliments or play coy with anyone.

"I can't believe I'm the last single sibling in the family," she said, smiling, before sadness flickered in her eyes. "Well, if you don't count Nick, who isn't technically single yet. I'm still hoping something good will happen there."

"You never know." Though Alec had his doubts that anything positive would emerge from the current cinders of that marriage.

"I haven't had any dessert yet. Want to check out the table? I heard Aunt Sophie brought her—"

"Come on, Katy!" Her cousin grabbed Katy's

hand and yanked her toward the mass quickly forming on the dance floor. The band had apparently taken a break, and Greek music began blasting from speakers flanking the floor. "It's your favorite!"

Katy sent Alec a laughing shrug and shouted, "Come with us!" before she joined the circle that snaked around the floor. He had to smile. He'd been dragged to participate a number of times in his life the same way Katy had been just now, and while he'd never learned the steps of various dances to be particularly proficient at them, he could usually muddle along and fake it.

Unlike Nick, who was the real deal when it came to Greek dancing. As the line of dancers gyrated, he led the group, hand in the air holding a kerchief, his graceful turns seemingly effortless. And he supposed it was effortless for Nick, since the man had learned them literally at his father's knee and practiced for years.

His attention slid from Nick to Katy again. She, too, knew Greek dancing like she could do it in her sleep. Watching her as she held hands with those on either side of her, as she stepped in and out in one of the intricate patterns, it struck him how amazingly graceful she was.

Klutzy Katy? Not this woman. Not the woman who, with a wide, encouraging smile, helped the guest to her left whose hand she held, a guest who was even less adept at Greek dancing than he was. This wedding was a break from the extreme fatigue of an intern, and she simply radiated energy.

Had he ever really watched her like this? Ever noticed her proud posture and delicate footsteps as she danced? Ever noticed how slim and shapely her ankles were as she gave little kicks and circled the room in the strappy high heels she wore?

Entranced, he watched her approach his side of the floor. To his surprise, she dropped her cousin's hand and grabbed his as she swept by, and he had no choice but to join the controlled chaos on the dance floor.

"Opa!" She grinned, any resemblance to studious Katy completely gone, replaced by this vibrant and exciting woman. Her hand was warm, nearly hot, as it clutched his. "You re-

member this one—it's the syrtos, one of the easi-
est," she said encouragingly, slightly breathless.
Damned if it wasn't obvious that the tables had
turned, and she'd become the teacher to the student. And what had changed her mind about
that, when she'd been so clearly unwilling before? "One, two, three, four, five, six, seven,
back, then again."

"I've only done this a couple of times at your
family's weddings, remember?"

"Surely a brilliant surgeon can do a little Greek
dance," she said in a teasing voice. "Just follow
my footsteps and you'll do fine."

He tried his best to follow her lead, shaking
his head as he messed up, yet feeling exhila-
rated, too, her hand clutched in his, her blue eyes
laughing. The music pounded across the floor
for what seemed like forever, and he felt his tension fade away, replaced by the simple pleasure
of dancing with her. Finally, the music stopped,
and everyone moved from the floor, catching
their breath as the band returned to play popu-
lar dance music.

"Whew! That was a workout. But you did

great!" Katy turned to him, her face flushed and dewy from exertion. Without warning, she flung her arms around his neck and gave him a smacking kiss on the lips.

Shocked, he stared into her laughing blue eyes and couldn't resist wrapping his arms around her, just like he had long ago. Unlike in the past, though, their embrace created a cyclone of emotion in his chest that threatened to burst out. The same emotion he'd felt both times he'd kissed her at the hospital. Emotion that nearly had him kissing her again right there in front of everyone at the reception.

He folded her close against his chest, savoring the moment. Let his lips touch her temple, slip to her soft cheek and linger there, before he forced himself to loosen his arms. To step back and shove his hands in his pockets before he did something he'd regret. Like grab her hand and pull her to his room and beg her to make love with him the rest of the night.

Her eyes had closed and she slowly opened them, her gaze holding his, and he wasn't sure what he saw within that beautiful blue. He just knew he wanted to keep looking there.

"YiaYia brought her famous kourambiethes. How about we get a few?"

"Sounds good." He knew he should find an excuse not to. But all he wanted was to spend a few more minutes with her. And what was the harm after all? They weren't at the hospital, around eyes that might judge them for talking together.

He let his hand rest against her back, touching her soft skin where the dress dipped low. They walked to the dessert table where the powdered-sugar-covered cookies were nestled in fluted paper cups.

"I'm betting you'll eat two," Katy said, as she put several on a plate.

"And I'm betting the extra one is really for you. As I recall, you had the biggest sweet tooth of the family."

"I admit nothing. I'm a doctor, so of course I only eat healthy foods." She grinned at him and grasped his hand, and damned if it didn't feel absolutely right for their palms to be pressed together.

Katy led them to a darkened corner of the ballroom and slipped the plate of cookies onto a tall, empty table. Her slender fingers picked up one of the cookies and held it to his mouth. "Remember not to do what you did last time you ate these," she said. The teasing tone had returned to her voice, her eyes twinkling with mischief.

God, he loved this Katy—the fun and relaxed woman who, outside the hospital work setting, couldn't be more adorable.

"What did I do last time I had these? Something stupid?"

"Not stupid. A rookie mistake. Inhaling while eating one, then the powered sugar makes you choke like crazy."

"Ah, yes, it's coming back to me." He grinned, remembering her teenage fists pounding on his back when the sugar had stuck in his lungs. "You almost injured my kidneys, whomping on my back like you did. It wasn't like I needed the Heimlich maneuver. What exactly did you think it would accomplish to assault me like that?"

"I guess it was silly." He liked her smile, both guilty and amused. "All us kids did that to one another whenever it happened, though there's clearly no medical reason for it. Maybe it was just an excuse to pound on one another. Sorry."

"Never be sorry." He couldn't resist running his finger down her cute nose. "Pretend to be confident, no matter what, and people will believe you are."

"Is this the secret to your success?" she asked, taking a bite of the cookie.

"I'm not sure I should share my secrets with you." In fact, he knew he shouldn't. The secret about his past that weighed on his present. That made it imperative he not think about Katy the way he couldn't stop thinking about her.

But as he stood close to her like this, seeing her lips covered with powdered sugar, he wanted more than anything to cover her mouth with his once more. To taste the sweetness of her along with the sweetness of the cookie.

Her gaze dropped to his lips, as though she'd read his mind, and her fingertip lifted to stroke her bottom lip. To lick the crumb of almonds and sugar there. His breath grew short, his pulse kicked into a different rhythm at that seductively tempting mouth. At the way she looked at him. He was no inexperienced kid. And damn if her eyes didn't hold the same intense heat and want that tilted his world sideways.

As though drawn by some unseen force, his head lowered and his mouth touched hers. His tongue slipped lightly across her lower lip, tasting the sugary sweetness there. His hand on her back drew her close as they shared an excruciatingly slow, soft, mind-blowing kiss. Her fingers slipped up his chest to the sides of his neck, and he heard a low, throaty groan, not sure if it came from her or from him. The sound had him pulling her closer, sent him deepening the kiss, until the band striking up a loud tune cut through his sensual fog.

It was all he could do to loosen his hold, to pull his mouth from hers, to leave the seductively sweet taste of sugar and of Katy. Panting slightly, they stared into one another's eyes for a long moment until Katy breathed, "Wow."

"Yeah. Wow." And wow was an understatement. But what, exactly, was he supposed to do now? Unlike the last time they'd kissed at a wedding, he was the one who'd started it. Along with the two others he hadn't been able to resist at the hospital. But she'd been so upset five years ago when he'd told her anything between them would be all wrong, how was he supposed to deal with the reality that it truly was?

"Who knew a kourambiethes kiss could be so incredible?" Katy said, her eyes heated but smiling, too, and he huffed out a breath of relief.

"How many kourambiethes kisses have you had in your life?"

"Ah, that's for you to wonder. You're not the only one who isn't sure they should share their secrets."

He smiled and shook his head. How the hell was he supposed to resist her teasing smile and beautiful eyes and incredibly sexy lips?

He would because he had to. Any sexual relationship between them—and God knew he wanted that more than he wanted his next breath—was strictly against hospital policy. Hurting her reputation or her career was something he couldn't risk, no matter how much he wanted her.

He shoved his hands into his pockets and cleared his throat. "I'm going to find your Uncle Constantine. Haven't seen him for years, since he couldn't make it to Nick's wedding."

"Before you go, will you dance with me, Alec?" The band had struck up a slow, dreamy tune and Katy licked the last of the sugar from her lips. Her eyes, now, oh, so serious, held his. Eyes he kept getting lost in when he let himself forget.

"I've already Greek-danced until my feet hurt." Until her hand had felt like it belonged in his. Until her brilliant smile had filled his soul to overflowing.

Her hand slipped from his arm to his wrist and, without thinking, he slid his hand out of his pocket. Her fingers, slim and still warm, captured his. "Please? Just one dance? I promise not to bother you the rest of the night."

Bother him? If she meant bother as in torture him with dreams of her naked in his arms and in his bed, he was sure she'd be doing exactly that for the rest of the night.

He moved toward the swaying couples on the

floor, still holding her hand in his, anticipating the pleasure and torture it would be to dance with her. To let the scent of her warm perfume surround him, let his hand drift from her waist to the soft, exposed skin of her back, let the loose tendrils of her silky hair tickle his face.

"Alec! We thought you'd probably be here."

Alec turned and froze. Shocked to see his elegant mother and sophisticated-looking father standing there, holding glasses of champagne in their hands. "Mom. Dad. I thought you were in Russia."

"Just got back this morning, which is why we didn't make the ceremony. Staying home a short time before we head back," his father said.

"We spotted you over in the corner with your… friend. Can you introduce us?" His mother's eyebrows were slightly raised as she looked at Katy, an intrigued expression on her face.

Alec realized with sudden, sickening clarity that he was holding Katy's hand, tucked closely against him. And he remembered extremely well the long, intense kiss they'd shared.

Dropping her hand like he'd been bitten by

a snake, he turned to look at Katy. That small frown he'd become accustomed to seeing dove between her brows again as her eyes scanned his face, and he wondered what the hell his expression looked like. He swallowed hard before he addressed his parents. "You remember Katy. Katherine Pappas. Nick's sister."

"Nick's baby sister? Why, I wouldn't have recognized you!" His mother shook Katy's hand. "What are you doing these days?"

"I just graduated from medical school and am interning at Oceancrest Medical Center."

"Interning at Oceancrest?" Charles Armstrong narrowed his gaze at his son, and Alec's gut clenched. He knew exactly what was coming next. "Are you an idiot, Alec? Cuddling up and dancing with a student from your hospital? Don't you ever learn?"

Alec set his jaw. Years of experience had taught him not to respond to his father's insults, and he certainly wouldn't react the way he wanted to. Not in the middle of a damned wedding reception. "Contrary to what you've always believed, I'm not an idiot. And what I do is my own business."

"Then don't be expecting me to bail you out again. I mean it."

"I never asked you to do that. Would never ask. And for what it's worth, Katy is like a sister to me." Which was a damned lie. Except he knew he had to double his efforts to remind himself that was all there could be between them. "If you'll excuse me, Katy and I were about to go talk with her Uncle Connie."

He turned and didn't even look to see if Katy was coming along or not. Hopefully not, because the last thing either of them needed was more speculation about their relationship. Then he realized she hadn't followed him at all…that she'd found someone else to dance with.

CHAPTER NINE

HER SHIFT THANKFULLY over after twelve hours, Katy headed to the changing room, grateful to put on real clothes for what seemed like the first time all week. She felt physically and mentally exhausted. Emotionally, too. Today was the anniversary of her father's death. It was the one day of the year she allowed herself to mourn and be sad. The distance between her and Alec added to the heaviness in her chest.

The heaviness had been weighing there since the wedding. Just as the two of them had been about to dance, after they'd shared a kiss so sweet she'd nearly melted to the floor, he'd yanked his hand from hers like she was a leper. Told his parents he thought of her as a sister, and the words had felt like he'd jammed his fist in her solar plexus.

The man had kissed her three times, damn it.

Wouldn't any woman think that meant he wasn't thinking of her as a "sister"? Player or no player, she had to believe Alec didn't kiss every woman he met before turning as cold as the proverbial cucumber and running away. Then again, history had shown she was very capable of deluding herself when it came to Alec Armstrong.

It had been a week since Dr. Boswell had taken over Alec's teaching rounds. Except for her current weariness, Katy felt like she was really finding her sea legs and not drowning in the hospital undertow. Dr. Boswell had proved to be a good teacher on rounds. Not as good as Alec, of course. But also not as distractingly attractive either.

She figured that had to be a good thing. Her goal was to learn how to be an excellent doctor, and being sidetracked as she noticed other things instead was a hindrance to that.

Noticed, for example, Alec's amazing bedside manner that engendered trust from even the most difficult patient. Diverted from listening to what patients had to say as he touched them with his long, beautifully shaped surgeon's hands. Engrossed by the vision of how incredibly sexy he looked in his green scrubs, his muscular chest and athletic tush filling them out in a way that would make any woman practically swoon.

She yanked off her scrub top and pulled on her sundress, thinking of how wonderful Alec had looked in his suit and tie at the wedding, how adorable he'd been, trying to Greek-dance. He'd seemed so much like the Alec she'd been getting to know again, teasing and fun and natural, and the memory of their kiss at the hospital had made her insides all warm and gooey. She'd felt a little Cinderella-like in her beautiful dress, dancing and eating with an oh-so-handsome prince then kissing him until she'd been breathless.

Then he'd just walked away, their planned dance apparently forgotten. Angry for deluding herself, she'd found someone else to dance with.

But then she'd seen him standing there, watching her. And the look on his face, a peculiar combination of fierceness and defeat and something she couldn't quite figure out, had brought back a small, budding hope that maybe she hadn't been wrong about him wanting her the way she wanted him.

With that tiny hope had come a tentative conviction. If presented with another opportunity to kiss him, she wasn't going to regret and wonder. She planned to be bold. To find out what might or might not be there between them.

She huffed out a long sigh. The unfortunate part of that plan was that she rarely saw Alec now. And today, of all the three-hundred-sixty-five days in the year, she would have loved to have his understanding support beside her. His presence would be a comfort, she knew, because it always had been.

Tears clogged her throat and she quickly swallowed to banish them. This year, the painful loss seemed even worse than it did most years. Her dad's absence at the wedding had left a sad emptiness in everyone's heart on an otherwise very happy day.

Nick understood a little. After all, it wasn't the best day of the year for him either. For some reason, though, they both seemed to want to handle it in their own ways. Separately, not together.

The door swung open and Elizabeth walked in and quickly stripped, throwing on her clothes like she was in a hurry. The fifth-year resident had seemed to thaw a little toward Katy, becoming nearly friendly since Dr. Boswell had taken over the teaching rounds. Katy didn't know what had motivated the change but was glad of it.

"You coming over to the Flat-Foot Tavern for liver rounds?" Elizabeth asked as she pulled a beaded shirt over her head.

"Liver rounds?"

"Yeah. Those of us off duty and not on call drink until our livers complain." Elizabeth grinned. "There'll be cute guys there from other services you might not have met yet. It's a fun break after a long week, and a good way to get to know people out of the hospital."

"I don't think I'm really in the mood to socialize."

"Suit yourself." Elizabeth shrugged. "But I'm heading over if you end up changing your mind."

Katy thought about her plan for the night. Which was to go to Nick's house and look through old family photo albums. Laugh and cry, then put them away for another year. Is that what her dad would want her to do?

No. He'd be so proud of her for getting through these first weeks of her internship, and even having a few successes. He'd want her to celebrate that. Make new friends. Maybe Alec would even be there, and her spirits would be lifted just by being with him, the way they'd always been.

"You know what? Mind's changed. I'm in."

Alec finished up the last of the paperwork on his desk, glad that this hell of a long day was finally over. He closed his eyes and let his head drop back against his chair, disgusted with himself that he'd had the gall to think he'd had a bad day. This latest news about a patient he'd liked and cared about, a patient whose family he'd become close with, was a painful blow. And he knew that, as painful as the sad prognosis for this man was for Alec, it was nothing compared to how it affected the man's wife and children.

His own unpleasant day had started with a phone call from his father in the morning, before his parents had left to go back to Russia for another week or two. The man had felt a need to ream Alec out yet again for his lack of good judgment and general failings as a doctor and human being.

Then Margaret Sanders had stopped by his office to talk about which fifth-year residents he would recommend being offered a permanent position. Talking with Margaret had made him think about nearly kissing Katy on the beach, which the CMO would have seen all too clearly if he had. Then thought about the times he had kissed her, and how much he wanted to do it again. Starting with her mouth and working his way down every inch of her beautiful body.

Damn it, he knew he couldn't act on this intense, nagging desire for her, but didn't need a constant reminder of that reality.

Or maybe the truth was he did need it. Should, in fact, welcome it. He couldn't ever make the same mistake again, no matter how much he wanted to. He could not risk Katy's reputation. Her future. And since he couldn't, avoiding her as much as possible was the least torturous solution to the attraction that felt inescapable.

He'd felt terrible after he'd walked away from her at the wedding. Then a different emotion— jealousy—had stabbed even deeper when she'd just moved on to dance with someone else. Though he sure couldn't blame her for that, since he couldn't be with her the way he wanted to be.

The deep breath he pulled into his lungs didn't calm the disquiet he felt. What he needed was a long run to clear his mind before the sun set. He knew running wasn't going to push the tragic news about his patient from his mind. Definitely wouldn't erase thoughts of Katy. Not thinking about her had proved impossible, but it had gotten slightly easier since he no longer saw her every day on teaching rounds.

Damn it, though, he missed her. Missed seeing her warm bedside manner. Missed seeing that little crease in her forehead as she pondered a problem. Missed seeing the desire in her eyes that mirrored his own, making not kissing her impossible.

He nearly groaned when his phone rang in his pocket, wondering how he'd get through another surgery in his current state of mind, until he remembered he wasn't on call tonight. He looked at it, relieved to see it was Nick. "What's up?"

"I need you to do a favor for me. Are you able to go to the Flat-Foot Tavern tonight?"

He stared at his phone. Nick's favor was to go to a bar? "Why?"

"Katy's there with the crew. I'd hoped to join her and keep her out of trouble, but I just got called in for an emergency surgery and can't."

"Why do you need to keep her out of trouble?" Of all the people he knew, Alec couldn't imagine Katy whooping it up and getting drunk and out of control.

"Today's the anniversary of Dad's passing. It sure as hell doesn't feel like he's been gone four years, does it?" Nick sighed in his ear. "You know how tough that was on all of us, but especially Katy. She was his baby, you know?"

"I know." His chest compressed in sympathy for the whole family, but he had a bad feeling he knew where this conversation was going. "What exactly are you asking me to do?"

"Katy usually stays home on this day and, basically, mourns. I expected to find her here, going through old family memorabilia, so I was surprised when she wasn't. Then she called and told me she was going to the bar. She's not a big drinker, and it doesn't take much for her to get looped. I'm afraid tonight might be the night she has a bit too much. To forget. And I can't be there to make sure she gets home okay."

Hell. "All right. I'll go."

"Thanks, Alec. I appreciate it."

A peculiar sensation rolled around in his chest. A strange combination of trepidation and anticipation at spending time with Katy, of being there for her. Thinking how much it would mean to him to be with her tonight as much as she might need him around.

He glanced at his watch. Just after nine. Surely it was too early for her to already be tipsy. Except liver rounds usually started around seven, so who knew?

He stacked the papers he'd signed, put them in his out-box and stood, ready to head out the door. Until he realized he needed a quick shower and to change into street clothes. And never mind that half the people at the Flat-Foot would be there straight after work, wearing scrubs.

Twenty minutes later he headed outside and across the street to the tavern as the sun dipped beneath the horizon. Even with the low light inside the bar, his gaze was instantly drawn to her. Katy.

He hadn't seen her for days, and he let himself stand there a moment to absorb the sight of her. Her hair gleaming, her smile surprisingly wide for a woman who was supposed to be feeling sad today. Laughing and bright-eyed and clinking a glass with some intern he hadn't met yet.

He remembered her trying to clink her glass with his, dumping her wine in his lap, and touching him until he'd nearly exploded. Good thing he'd arrived to make sure she didn't have the same effect on the young guy, and never mind that it shouldn't be any of his business.

He weaved through the crowded tables, the thump of the bass music seeming to pound a primal rhythm into his body. He pulled up a chair next to Todd Eiterman, the second-year surgical resident. Close to Katy, but not so close as to raise eyebrows. Though eyebrows were raised anyway, since he didn't make a habit of doing liver rounds with the residents.

"Any lives saved today?" he asked, to make small talk, looking around the table of hard-working young doctors relaxing after a long week. Hoping no one saw him looking particularly closely at Katy, trying to see if she'd been drinking much. Trying not to think about how good it would feel to drape his arm across her shoulders. To feel her soft skin beneath his hand that was exposed by the spaghetti-strapped sundress she wore.

"Every day, Dr. Armstrong. Every day." Elizabeth smiled coyly and lifted her glass of wine.

Alec didn't have a glass to lift, so he simply gave her a return half-smile. "Good. Cheers."

"Here, Alec. I mean Dr. Armstrong. Toast with this—I'm going to get another one." Katy held her glass out to him. Her mostly empty glass, and what had been inside it, he wasn't sure. Margarita? Daiquiri?

He didn't want her drink, but he also didn't want her to be drinking it either. It was more than obvious from the over-brightness of her eyes and the slight slur to her words that she'd already had plenty. He felt an urge to sweep her up and out of there before she embarrassed herself, but forced himself to be patient. To wait for the right moment when it wouldn't seem like a big deal.

He held up the glass. "Cheers, everyone. You're all doing a great job."

The cheer was loudly chorused, and he took a sip to be polite. Margarita, and a strong one, at that. How many had she had?

He looked at Katy again, but her face was turned to Elizabeth next to her. Within the loud beat of the music in the bar, he couldn't hear her words, so he just let himself study her profile. Her cute little nose and generous lips. Her slender hands fingering the necklace slipping down between the hint of her breasts that peeked from the top of her dress. He found his breath growing short, wished he could replace her hand with his own to stroke that delicate skin. Then figuratively smacked himself for the thought.

Damn. He took a swig of her drink, grimaced

a little since he didn't particularly like margaritas, and pretty much emptied the already nearly empty glass. He answered questions and engaged in chitchat while half his mind wondered how he was going to discreetly get her out of there without anyone noticing.

Katy stood, clearly wobbly on her feet, and picked up her purse as she turned, likely to go to the restroom. This was his chance to talk with her alone and get her home. The waitress stopped at the table, and Katy sent Alec a wide smile. "Alec, let me buy you a drink. I'm having another one."

Like hell she was. Time to scrap the idea of being discreet. "I can't stay. And unfortunately you can't either because your brother asked me to drive you home."

"I don't need a driver. I have my car here."

"Except you're not driving it."

"Says who? Besides, I'm not ready to leave."

Alec nearly laughed at the look she gave him, which could only be described as a death glare, coupled with a deep frown. Apparently the normally sweet and apologetic Katy had another side that was unleashed after a few drinks. Or, he considered, she might still be ticked about the way he'd left her at the dance floor.

"I'll make sure she gets home, Dr. Armstrong," Todd said.

He looked at the young man, who seemed sober enough. But he'd promised Nick he'd see her safely home. At that moment Katy turned and stalked—if you could call her wobbly gait stalking—to the restroom, and Alec exhaled in relief. This was his chance.

"Thanks, Todd. That would be great. I'll see you all later." He headed toward the door then pivoted back toward the restroom. Out of the corner of his eye he saw one person was still watching him. Elizabeth.

Damn it. Caught.

No matter. He was going to get Katy out of there without a scene, text Todd that he'd driven her after all and fulfill his duty.

Duty? Who was he kidding? This had nothing to do with duty and everything to do with the surge of protective instinct he was feeling.

That, for whatever reason, he'd always felt toward Katy.

After what seemed like an eternity the door to the women's restroom finally swung open. She tripped over her heel and stumbled into him, grasping his arms as he steadied her against his chest.

"Oh! Sorry." Her big blue eyes blinked up at him, and that scowl settled on her face again. "Oh. It's you. Why do you and Nick seem to think I need taking care of? I don't need a babysitter. I'm a big girl now. I can take care of myself."

"I know you can. But you've had too much to drink to drive, and I think you know that."

She stared up at him, now with just that tiny frown between her brows that was such a cute part of who she was. Did she know her fingers moved on the skin of his arms, caressingly, tantalizingly, as they stood so close to one another in the dark, narrow hallway? His hands tightened on her shoulders, and he forced himself to loosen them.

"Okay." Her breasts rose and fell in a deep

sigh. "I know I shouldn't drive. But I...I don't want to go home. Not just yet."

"Fine. We'll go somewhere else." How could he insist he take her home when her eyes looked so clouded and sad, when her lips trembled ever so slightly? He needed to take her mind off the pain of losing her dad. Off the stress of work. Off anything but simple pleasures.

He shoved down thoughts of the kind of pleasure he'd really like to offer her, and decided on where he could take her. Somewhere sure to bring the smile to her face that he needed to see again. "Let's go to my place and take a walk along the bay to clear our heads."

"That sounds good." Already the clouds in her eyes were fleeing, and Alec's heart felt a little lighter as he led her out the side door of the tavern.

Moonlight lit the lapping water of the bay as he swung his car into the driveway of his condo. Katy had been uncharacteristically quiet the entire ride. He turned the ignition off and looked at her, so close in the seat next to him. The sadness that was back in her eyes knocked the air from his chest.

"Come on. Something's happening soon I want you to see. Something that will make you smile."

"I don't feel much like smiling today."

"I know. To be honest, I don't either. But maybe we can find a reason to smile together." He walked to her side of the car and opened the door, reaching for her soft hand. "It's a little chilly, so wear your sweater." She'd need the light warmth, and it would be good to see less of her smooth skin that tempted him to touch it.

He led her down to the bike path that circled the bay, holding her hand because she was still a little unsteady on her feet. And because it just felt right to twine his fingers with hers. It would've seemed oddly distant to just walk side by side with her, when both of them could use the warmth and comfort of that small connection. After all, it wasn't as though some spy from the hospital was watching.

The simple act of strolling with her, the crisp night air in his lungs, the moon hanging in the starry sky, all seemed to clear his mind of everything that had weighed him down that day. He looked at Katy and hoped she felt a little of that, too. "I'm sorry about your dad. I know him being gone is hard on all of you."

"Things like a family wedding are a sad reminder, you know?" She looked up at him, and even through the darkness he could see the shadows in her eyes, a misting of tears that clutched at his heart. "He would've loved to live long enough to see a first grandchild and be a wonderful *papou*. He would've loved to see Elena married. He would've been so happy to see me graduate from med school. It...it really breaks my heart he never got to do any of those things."

He stopped walking to cup her cheek with his free hand. Wipe away the single tear that had escaped her brimming eyes and squeezed his heart. "I know. Life isn't fair, is it?"

She shook her head. "No. It definitely isn't. He gave me this necklace to remind me to always go after what I wanted. I wear it every day and can feel him with me."

Her eyes held wistful sadness as she fingered the necklace. Alec wanted to offer her comfort, to hold her, kiss her, until there was only happiness in their sapphire depths. But he couldn't. He could only offer words. "Your dad was proud of all of his kids, but I think you were special to him. You shared his love of puzzles and mysteries. I remember how much he got a kick out of the backward solutions you came up with when everyone else only thought forward."

"He did, didn't he?" The smile that touched her lips was small, but it was a start. "So tell me why you don't feel much like smiling today either."

Should he tell her? He rarely shared when he was upset about a patient. But she'd shared with him, so it was only fair that he open a little of himself up to her, too.

"A few years ago, I had a patient with colon cancer. I got to know him well, and his family, too. He's just a great person, as is his wife. They have three of the cutest kids." He sucked in a breath, thinking how they'd all been sure the worst health problems were over for the man. "I performed a hemicolectomy on him, then he had a course of chemotherapy, and he's been doing well until this week when he started having stomach pain. Today we found out the cancer has spread to his liver." He could still see the man's wife's tears, the way they'd clutched each other when he'd had to tell them the bad news. And damn if that wasn't the absolute hardest part of his job.

"I'm sorry." It was her turn to squeeze his hand, and he was surprised that telling her, and having her listen, felt good. "I haven't had to go through that yet, but I know I will have to help patients deal with bad news when I'm in a family practice. I hope I do okay."

"You don't have to hope. You have a wonderful way with patients. I've seen it firsthand and have had quite a few people tell me, too."

"Really?" This time a real smile touched her face, which made him smile, too. "That's good to hear. Thank you."

The first boom sounded in the air, and Katy stopped walking. "What was that?"

"What I brought you out here to see. What I said would make you smile."

More loud booms, and then red, green and white sparkles lit the night sky.

"Fireworks?"

"From the adventure park. You can see them across the bay."

"Oh! They're beautiful!"

He watched her face and was filled with a feeling of triumph when he saw her eyes light almost as brightly as the fireworks. As her smile grew wider she gasped with delight. And damned if the soft sound, the expression of pleasure on her face, didn't make him wonder how she would look, how she would sound, as he buried his nose in her soft neck and buried himself in her beautiful body.

He shouldn't think those kinds of forbidden thoughts, but he just couldn't escape the fierce desire for her that had become a constant, intense ache.

He turned, not wanting to look at her. Not wanting to see her shining eyes and lush lips and her curves hidden beneath her dress that kept giving him these insane thoughts. Thoughts that gnawed at him. Thoughts of taking her to his condo and stripping off her clothes and making love with her all night.

No. He had to suppress it. And since he didn't seem to be able to accomplish that out here with the bright, silvery moonlight touching her hair and skin and smile, he had to end the evening and take her home. He took a few steps away, back toward the car.

"Nick will be wondering where you are." His voice came out gruff, hoarse, but it was the best he could do. "And I have an early morning tomorrow." It wasn't true. In fact, he had the day off. But a little lie was nothing if it helped him get her home before he did something he'd regret. That they'd both regret.

"Alec."

He looked back at her and, to his shock, she was right there. Inches away. His breath backed up in his lungs at the expression on her face.

It wasn't sad any more, or worried or studious or any of the things he was used to seeing on her lovely face. It was determined. And sensual. A combination that both excited and alarmed him.

"Yes?" he asked, wary, his heart beating

harder, the excitement and alarm growing as she closed the small gap between them.

In answer, she rose up on her toes, wrapped her arms around his neck and pressed her mouth to his.

CHAPTER TEN

Alec stood there motionless, as though he were a statue, as she kissed him. He didn't pull away, but didn't participate either. She'd known he'd be surprised, but she'd had to taste him. Had to kiss him one more time.

His lips were so warm, so soft. She ran her tongue across the seam of them, and was rewarded as he opened them slightly, as his tongue touched hers, and she drank in the taste of him.

His hands closed around her shoulders, tightened, and with a strange, strangled sound in his throat he seemed to give in. Tilted his head and opened his mouth over hers. Brought her body tightly against his. It felt so right, so wonderful, to be pressed so closely to his heart she could feel the pounding of it against her breasts.

His stiff form loosened, molded to hers, hip to hip and thigh to thigh. His hands left her shoulders to wrap around her back, his fingers digging slightly into her flesh as his mouth devoured hers. As though he was starving for her in exactly the same way she'd been starving for him.

Yes. Yes. Yes. The mantra broke through the fogginess of her brain. Each kiss before this had gotten longer, sweeter. Now they were sharing the kind of passion she'd dreamed of. She arched up, kissing him more boldly now, letting her fingers thread into his soft hair, the thick waves curving around her fingers, holding onto her. Her holding on to him.

Abruptly, his arms dropped from her back, his hands grasped her shoulders again, and he set her away from him. His chest heaved in deep breaths. Her stomach tightened as it became clear, even through the darkness, that his expression wasn't smiling and sensual. It was very serious.

"Katy. I'm sorry. I shouldn't have kissed you in the hospital and again at the wedding. I shouldn't have kissed you now."

"It's not for you to be sorry." She tilted her chin

at him, refusing to let him take the blame. Trying to push down the regret she, too, felt. Not regret for the kiss. Regret that he wouldn't allow himself to be with her the way she so wanted him to be. "I kissed you, not the other way around."

"This time, maybe. But that still makes it three to one." His serious expression gave way to a glimmer of a smile.

"Actually, it's three to two, counting the time I kissed you five years ago."

"Okay, Miss Math. Though I didn't think you liked to remember that kiss too much."

"I don't. Do you have any idea how embarrassed I felt when you turned me down flat and ran away like a dog being chased by a cat?"

"I'm sorry. I was most definitely a dog that night." He lifted his hand to her hair, blowing in the breeze, and tucked it behind her ear. His fingers slowly continued down to stroke her cheekbone. "But I think you know now it wasn't because I wasn't attracted to you. Which, to my astonishment, I was that day."

"And now?"

"Now I'm beyond attracted to you." Even in

the darkness she could see his eyes grow serious again as he cupped her face in his hand. "But I can't do anything about it."

"Why?"

"You know why. You're a student and I'm an attending physician. Your teacher. It's not ethical."

"You're not my teacher any more. Dr. Boswell is."

"It doesn't matter. People love to talk—you know that. I couldn't bear to have you gossiped about, maybe even have your career jeopardized. Nick and I even worried about people calling favoritism just because you're his sister. Believe me, I know how it can be. We can't do this, no matter how much I want to."

"How much do you want to?" she asked. Wondering if it could possibly be as much as she did.

"You want a demonstration?" His eyes glinted. "Something you can quantify, Miss Science? Then here it is." He pulled her tightly against him, angled his mouth to hers, and kissed her hard. Fiercely and possessively and without reserve. A kiss that most definitely beat out all their prior kisses tenfold. A kiss that sent her heart racing and hot tingles surging through every nerve and was everything she'd dreamed for years and years that kissing him would be.

Katy clutched his shirt with her hands. A moan formed in her throat as his hot mouth explored hers so deeply and thoroughly that her knees wobbled beneath her. Then nearly stumbled as he released her and backed away. A chill replaced the warmth that had spread across her body on every inch they'd touched each other.

"Does that give you something to measure?" The dark eyes that stared at her glittered with a passion that shortened her breath even more. "I want you, Katy. I think about you all day long. Wondering if I'm going to run into you in some patient's room or the hallway or the lunchroom. I look for you, even though I tell myself not to. Even though I've tried hard not to. I want you, but we can't do this. I won't be responsible for damaging your career."

"No one has to know. No one will know."

"A dangerous assumption to make."

He grasped her hand and began to walk back

toward his car, so quickly that she stumbled in her heels and he slowed down. "I'm taking you home now."

He'd told her he wanted her. Thought of her all day long. Just as she did him. But the huge problem keeping them apart couldn't be ignored, and she knew it. She didn't want her career damaged any more than he did. How could she be the doctor her father had been if she let her personal life cloud her judgment? A secret affair with a man who was technically her boss was not something her father would have wanted for her—even if that man was Alec. And she understood why he didn't want to go through that again either.

As they'd both said earlier, life wasn't fair. And that reality felt like a brick on her heart.

"Can I see your apartment before you take me home? Maybe have a quick cup of coffee?" She wasn't quite ready to say goodbye. Knew a cup of coffee wouldn't really make a difference but grasped at any reason to spend just a few more minutes with him.

He looked down at her, his expression now unreadable. "You want coffee?"

"Yes. Please."

He looked at her a long moment, so long she nearly fidgeted beneath his gaze, before he finally led her into his condo. Floor-to-ceiling windows looked over the starlit bay from his living room, which was furnished with modern pieces in clean, sleek lines. They moved into a spacious kitchen with gleaming appliances and a huge island with bar stools on one side. "Have a seat at the counter. You'll see there's a plate of kourambiethes your *yiayia* insisted I bring home with me."

Mmm…kourambiethes. Instantly, she remembered the powdered sugar on his lips as it had been at the wedding, and knew she'd never again eat one again without thinking of him.

He had one of those single-cup coffee-brewing machines, and placed a steaming cup in front of her before brewing one for himself. She looked at his strong back, his shoulders broad in the blue polo shirt he wore tucked into the waistband of jeans. Watched his long, surgeon's fingers nimbly work the machine.

Why couldn't she feel those talented fingers, just once, touching her everywhere? Feel his skin and muscles under her own hands? Knowing he wanted her the way she wanted him but that they couldn't let it happen made her chest ache even more than when he'd rejected her five years ago.

Welcoming the distraction of hot coffee with a sweet cookie, she picked up one of the kourambiethes and handed it to Alec, then took one for herself. She took a bite then realized he was looking at her mouth. Watching her eat, his eyelids low, his eyes dark. She ran her tongue slowly across her sugary lip, deliberately tempting him. What could be wrong with one last, sweet kiss?

Still staring at her, he took a bite of cookie, and his chest lifted as he drew a breath.

Suddenly he began to choke. Lord, it was the powdered sugar! She jumped off the stool and ran to the other side of the counter, pounding on his back with her fists as his body was wracked by a violent cough.

ROBIN GIANNA 191

"Ow, damn it, stop!" His eyes watered as he choked and coughed and finally got his breathing under control. He turned and grabbed her wrists. "Geez, Katy! Didn't we already talk about the medical necessity for this? Or are you just mad and trying to kill me?"

"Trying to kill you, I guess. Haven't you heard about hell and the fury of a woman scorned? But if you kiss me, I'll spare you."

One more kiss. Was that so much to want? She pressed her hands, her wrists still imprisoned in his hands, against his chest. His heart beat hard against her palms. Harder than it should have been just from his choking episode. As hard as hers currently pounded in her own chest.

"Katy." His eyes were dark and hot. His voice low and rough. "It's nearly impossible for me to resist kissing you as it is. Now you have to add a threat of bodily harm?"

"Just trying to even up the score. Which is currently four to two." She leaned up to press her mouth to his, softly, slowly, not wanting to be accused of assaulting him again. Just wanting to taste him. Wanting him to feel what was between them.

His warm lips moved with hers for a long moment until he broke the kiss. "Does everything have to be a competition with you? How about letting me win this? Leave it at three to four?"

"I don't think so. I'm liking this kissing contest a lot." She kissed him again, and he tasted beyond wonderful, a spicy hint of coffee mixed with sugar and him.

He pulled his mouth from hers, his hands tighter on her wrists now. Tension emanated from him, and heat, too. His eyes glittered, most definitely a wild, tiger-eye color as he stared at her, and she could see very clearly that his need was every bit as powerful as her own. "So now we're even. Are you happy?"

"Yes. I'm happy. But I could be happier." She pulled her wrist loose from his hold and grasped his hand. Brought his palm to her breast and held it there. His fingers tightened, his thumb sweeping across her nipple, and it felt so wonderful she gasped.

"Damn it, you don't play fair," he said in a low growl, still stroking her breast.

"All's fair in love and war." She used her free hand to tug part of his shirt from his pants, slipping her fingers beneath until she could feel him tremble.

"Is this love or war?" His hot breath slipped across her cheeks as his lips caressed her face.

"Maybe a little of both."

"Yeah." The word came out on a groan as he released her other wrist, wrapped his arm around her back and kissed her. No longer teasing and soft. This was a real kiss, deep and hot and nearly desperate, and she sank into it as one hand caressed her breast, the other sliding down to squeeze her bottom.

"Katy." The word came against her lips as he kissed her, delved deeply again, their tongues dancing together as he claimed her mouth for his own. The countertop pressed into her lower back as he molded his body to hers. She wound her arms around his neck and held on, feeling the tension in the muscles of his shoulders, in the tautness of his body. Her knees felt so weak she thought she just might slither to the floor.

"Katy," he said again, his voice ragged, his eyes dark. He gave her a small smile as he imperceptibly shook his head. "I'm going to hell for this, you know." Then he kissed her again.

A feeling of relief swept through her as she realized they'd both finally, finally surrendered to the force that was clearly bigger than both of them. His kiss was filled with passion and sweetness but no regret. Only want.

She brought her hands to his waist, tugging his shirt loose to feel his skin, his body. His muscles shivered beneath her palms as she stroked under his shirt.

He responded by pulling the straps of her dress off her shoulders, tugging more until it hung at her waist and her lacy bra was all that covered her breasts. With his agile fingers, he quickly flicked the clasp and slid it, too, from her arms.

"I've fantasized for more hours than you can imagine how your breasts look." His voice was hoarse as he looked at her. "Do you know how beautiful you are?"

"What I know is that I don't know exactly how beautiful you are," she said. She wanted to see him, look at him the way he was looking at her. She pulled his shirt up and off. Her breath caught at the width of his shoulders, at the muscled strength of his chest, at the fine layer of dark hair covering it. She smoothed her hands up and over all of it, loving the feel of him against her palms. Wanting the feel of all of him against all of her.

He grabbed a cookie from the plate on the counter, his eyes gleaming. "Promise not to bruise me again if I choke?"

"I— Oh...!"

All thought of how she was going to respond left her brain when he rubbed the cookie slowly across and around one nipple, then the other, his mouth following to lick and suck the sugar left behind. The feel of his lips and tongue were so magical and wildly erotic she could barely breathe. She tangled her fingers in his thick hair, held him to her, and moaned.

With his mouth still on her breasts, he pulled her dress the rest of the way down her body until she stood there wearing only her panties. He sank to his knees, his mouth continuing down, circling her navel. Moving lower until his lips and tongue pressed against the damp front of her underwear. She moaned again, melting for him.

Perhaps he sensed that her legs were about to crumple beneath the erotic invasion of his mouth, because he suddenly stood. His long, warm fingers grasped her bottom and lifted her to his waist before he began moving from the kitchen. She wrapped her legs around his hips and clung to his neck, kissing him, still able to taste a little of the sugar on his tongue.

"You taste unbearably sweet," he whispered between kisses. "Even without the sugar." He carried her into a bedroom, and her heart pounded so loudly in her ears it was like a drumbeat. Finally. Finally. But he passed the big bed and moved to a sliding glass door.

"Where are we going?" Surely he wasn't going to go all noble now after he'd made her crazy with wanting him. "I'm thinking a bed is a good idea. Like now."

"Who knew you could be so impatient?" He

grinned as he shoved open the door and stepped into the breezy night, onto a covered, private balcony accessed only from the bedroom. "Ever since you came to San Diego I've thought of you out here with me. Thought of how you would look, naked on the cushions of this chaise lounge with the breeze in your hair and the moonlight in your eyes."

He gently lowered her to the chaise and the bay breeze did tease across her nakedness, sensuous and wonderful, and she wanted him to feel the same thing. Needed him naked—now.

"You, too." She sat up and grasped the belt of his jeans, undid the buckle. "I want to see your body in the moonlight."

"Your wish is my command." His eyes crinkled at the corners, but in their depths was the same deep longing and desire that had filled her from the moment he'd kissed her on the bay. From the moment she'd first seen him again.

He stripped off his jeans, socks and underwear in a hurry, then settled his torso between her legs. Licked along the inside of her thigh as he pulled the last bit of her clothing down and off.

Kissed his way up her body as his hands gently stroked her legs, opening them, as he settled himself in between to nuzzle her neck and nip her earlobe.

"Too bad the fireworks are over," he said against the hollow of her throat. "We could have heard and seen them from here."

"I'm willing to bet we're going to make some fireworks of our own." There was no doubt about that as her body was already consumed by an intensely sparkling heat she'd never known existed.

He chuckled against her neck. "I won't take that bet, because my goal is to make you explode."

He kissed her again as his fingers found her core, touched her, caressed her, as her own fingers explored his smooth contours. His face, his shoulders, his tight buttocks, his back. Clasped him in her hand until both of them were gasping into one another's mouths, their bodies moving, skin against skin.

She'd dreamed of this for so long. Wanted this so long. Part of her wanted to savor every second, to draw out their lovemaking all night. But the part of her that wanted him beyond anything she'd ever experienced couldn't wait. She wrapped her legs around his hips, drew him in to join with her. They moved together, creating an instant rhythm of perfection between them, giving and taking until the moment couldn't be held off any longer. Her climax making her cry out, he covered her mouth with his, absorbing the sound as they both fell.

Alec lay propped on his elbow in his bed and watched Katy sleep, listening to her breathe as she lay on her back next to him. He gazed at her sweet face in repose, her eyelashes resting on her cheeks. At her motionless body, positioned as a sleeping fairy-tale princess would be, her hands one on top of the other resting on her belly, her beautiful hair in a thick halo of waves around her head. Deep in the kind of sleep only someone who'd been without it too long could have.

The breeze from his ceiling fan lifted strands of her hair, and he gently stroked them from her eyes and tucked them behind her ears. His chest filled and his gut tightened with too many swirling emotions.

Pleasure. Regret. Worry. Joy.

He shouldn't have let it happen. Hadn't been able to keep it from happening.

He let his finger trace her eyebrow, slip down her nose, touch her beautiful lips. Her face twitched in response, and he had to smile. She was a woman of contrasts, like no one he'd met before. So smart, someone who thought deeply and carefully, who took her job seriously, and yet who could be almost childlike at times in a charming and adorable way.

Katy. He'd never have dreamed when she'd tagged along after Nick and him all those years ago that he'd be lying in bed with her, sated, happy, content. He should get up. Leave her to get her much-needed rest as he went for a run, fixed some breakfast for both of them. Then take her home and hope to hell her brother had no clue why she'd really spent the night at his home.

All this was dangerous. So potentially damaging to both their careers. But as he looked at her, he knew he couldn't walk away and end it now.

He wanted to spend the day with her. Wanted to spend more time learning how her interesting mind worked. Wanted to explore the world through her eyes, which had always seen things a little differently than most.

He wasn't her teacher any more. And, yes, he knew it was a damned lame excuse for not breaking it off right now, before it had barely started. He wished he was strong enough, but he wasn't.

He could only hope and pray they wouldn't both regret heading down the path in front of them. The all-too-thrilling path that was also scary as hell.

CHAPTER ELEVEN

"HI, DR. BOSWELL. Dr. Armstrong." Could anyone tell her heart thumped absurdly fast as she tried to stand nonchalantly in the doctors' lounge by their lunch table? How hard it was to suppress a secret smile as she looked at Alec's handsome face? How hard it was to not reach out and smooth his slightly messy hair from his forehead?

"Hello, Dr. Pappas." The smile Alec gave back to her probably seemed normal enough to anyone watching. But Katy could see the glint deep in their amber depths that showed he was feeling exactly as she was. Still remembering their incredible and beautiful time together three nights ago. "Are you giving Dr. Boswell any trouble?"

"I'm trying not to. I don't think I've made any mistakes for at least a few hours."

"I think it's actually been an entire day." Dr.

Boswell chuckled. "In truth, Alec, our student is doing a stellar job. She's the kind of intern who makes teaching rounds a pleasure."

"She is indeed." That glint in his eyes grew a little hotter as their eyes met, which made Katy feel short of breath. He must have realized how he was looking at her as he seemed to quickly school his face into bland professionalism and turned back to Dr. Boswell. "I hope the interns I get next month work as hard as she and Michael Coffman have been."

Elizabeth Stark stopped next to her as she stood at the men's table, holding an empty lunch tray, her gaze a little cold as it slid over Katy, which surprised her. A slight chill of anxiety slid down her spine. Elizabeth had been so much friendlier the past week. Had the woman somehow picked up on the vibe between Alec and her?

Elizabeth shifted her attention to the two surgeons. "Dr. Boswell, are you still planning for me to do the appendectomy this afternoon?"

The man nodded. "Should be a cakewalk for you by now, Dr. Stark. I'm impressed with the skills you've shown me so far. You're just about ready to go off on your own."

"Thank you." She inclined her head in acknowledgement of the compliment as her face relaxed a bit into a pleased smile. Katy knew Elizabeth put tremendous pressure on herself to achieve in the surgical arena, which was still primarily a man's world. Another reason Katy was more than happy that she'd chosen family practice for her future.

Elizabeth turned to Katy. "When you're done with lunch, come find me. I have a few patients I need you to see."

"Okay. I won't be long." She wanted one more quick look at Alec. Wanted to be the recipient of another smile that lit his eyes. But knew she couldn't linger and possibly raise any red flags, so she looked at Dr. Boswell instead. "I'll be here if you need me. Otherwise I'll see you for rounds in the morning."

Katy moved to a table at the back of the room and faced the wall so she wouldn't be tempted to stare at Alec. After their amazing night and day together, she'd found it a little hard to concentrate when she'd first come back to work. Thankfully, she'd gotten back into the groove soon enough and was so busy working umpteen hours she didn't have time to think about anything but her patients.

Still, when she did have a free moment her mind instantly drifted to her wonderful day off. A day off that had seemed like far more than twenty-four hours. Probably, she thought, hoping the dreamy smile on her face wasn't obvious to the entire lunchroom, because she'd spent the day with Alec. A day filled with delicious love-making, laughter, and fun.

Kayaking on the bay, then lovemaking at Alec's place. Lunch by the ocean on Mission Beach, a little swimming, then back to his condo to make love. Sailing on Alec's small sailboat then making love again.

Could any day possibly have been any more perfect?

With a smile on her face she just plain couldn't suppress, she finished up her lunch. Alec had already left, and when she felt a twinge of disappointment sternly reminded herself that was a good thing. She contacted Elizabeth on the hospital call system to find out where she needed to be next.

"Twentieth floor. I have to be somewhere else in a few minutes, so I need you to get here quickly," Elizabeth responded. Was it Katy's imagination that her voice was a tad curt?

She hurried to the floor and found Elizabeth going over some charts. "What do you need from me?"

"That patient you tried to assassinate with potassium a couple weeks ago?" Elizabeth barely glanced up from the charts. "Like a boomerang, she's back again."

"Mrs. Patterson?" Katy frowned. "Why?"

"She actually was here a few days back when you were off work. Typical granny problems, but the nursing home sent her in anyway. She still had lactic acidosis, and the diagnosis was again ischemic colitis."

"So why is she back today?"

Elizabeth rolled her eyes. "Same old. Lactic acidosis again. In my opinion, she just has the dwindles and is depressed and nervous. Then the nursing home gets nervous, too, and sends her back. I remembered she liked you, so why don't you do her workup, see if you can reassure her before we send her back to the home?"

"Okay. I'll be glad to. Thanks." Katy took the chart and headed toward Mrs. Patterson's room. When she got there she stopped abruptly in the doorway, staring for a moment, shocked at what she saw.

"Helen?" She hurried to the woman's bedside. The woman looked astonishingly ill. Nothing at all like the energetic, chatty woman she'd been just weeks ago. How could she have lost so much weight in such a short period of time? She'd been the tiniest thing, anyway, when she'd been here before. Now she was practically skin and bones. She reached for the woman's hand. "Tell me what's going on."

"Who are you?" Her eyes had a hollow look to them as she peered at Katy, with none of the friendliness and vitality that had sparkled in them before.

Her words jerked Katy's heart. Was the woman delirious? "It's me, Katy Pappas. The intern. I took care of you the first time you came in. Just a couple weeks ago."

Helen stared at her, then gave a tiny nod. "Oh, yes. I remember."

Katy warmed her stethoscope, then listened to the woman's lungs and heart and took her pulse. "Tell me why you're here. How you're feeling."

"My stomach hurts so much. I can't eat. I don't sleep well." Her thin hand rested on Katy's. "I think it's my time. I think I'm dying."

"Not if I can help it." Katy pressed her lips together. This didn't sound like a normal post-op problem. Or simply ischemic colitis. Before her hip surgery Helen had been a very active, healthy woman. What could possibly be going on? "I'm going to check some things and see what we can figure out. Hang in there." She squeezed the poor woman's shoulder and headed to the computers to look at Helen's lab results. And hoped and prayed there would be one little thing that would shed light on this peculiar mystery.

Katy closeted herself in one of the hospital computer labs where she'd have some quiet to study and think. She pulled up all Helen Patterson's records. Her hip surgery. Tests done at that time and during her next admissions. She turned to the mnemonic used for studying the anion gap of metabolic acidosis—MUDPILES.

Ruling out several of the various causes for acidosis in the MUDPILES mnemonic was fairly easy, but still didn't give her an answer. Then she called on the training her dad had given her. The puzzle master. The ultimate mystery-solver.

Define the goal. The topic. What did she already know on the subject? Set aside the first, most obvious solutions and keep an open mind. Place the facts in a pattern she could understand and evaluate.

She stared at all the information on the computer, gnawing her lip. Think, Katy, think.

It almost seemed as though the type on the screen grew crisper, brighter, practically leaping out at her. The answer was right there. But what a crazy answer it was! Would anybody believe it? Who should she try to convince first?

Nobody. The first thing she had to do was prove her hunch, her conviction, through a blood test.

Sucking in a fortifying breath, she ordered the test and asked for the results to be determined STAT. Then managed to distract herself by seeing other patients, but checked every few minutes to see if the tests were done, practically jumping for joy when the results came in. Then stared in both triumph and disbelief.

Katy's heard thumped and her adrenaline flowed. She remembered Alec reminding her to look for the zebra while everyone else was looking for the horse. And, man, this zebra was a big one.

She turned from the computer, hands a little sweaty. She'd start with Alec. He'd advise her what to do and what steps had to be taken.

After what was only ten or so minutes but seemed like hours, Katy was able to find out where he was. And what could possibly make the elevators so painfully slow? Rushing through the corridors, she finally found Alec about to enter a patient's room and ran up to him.

"Dr. Armstrong! I need to speak with you right away."

A frown formed between his brows as he

looked at her then quickly glanced up and down the hall. He took a step back and spoke in a low voice. "Dr. Pappas. As you know, Dr. Boswell is covering teaching rounds now. You need to address any questions to him."

"No. I know." She gulped. Obviously, he thought she was here for personal reasons and was worried about hospital gossip. Didn't he know she fully understood they had to keep their distance here? "I have a very peculiar situation with a patient and I need to talk with you about it. Have you advise me, because we may have to get the police involved."

His expression turned to one of surprise. "All right. What's going on?"

"You remember Helen Patterson? The patient who accidentally got too much oral potassium on my first night on call?"

"Yes. I remember."

"She's been back two more times for ischemic colitis, which seemed a little strange to me. Then when I went to see her I couldn't believe how different she was, really sick-looking and a little confused."

He stared at her intently. "Go on."

"I set aside the most obvious answers then did some critical thinking. I saw there was one thing that hadn't been checked because normally there wouldn't be a reason to. So I ordered the test. It's confirmed. Her ethylene glycol levels are through the roof."

"What? How is that possible? She's been living in a nursing home."

"Here's the crazy part. Are you ready?" She prayed he'd believe her hypothesis. "I believe her son is poisoning her with antifreeze. He needs money—I know he's been borrowing plenty from her, and she told him she wouldn't give him any more. I know it seems...unbelievable, but my gut tells me it's true and the lab results support it."

He studied her, his eyes thoughtful, then gave a nod. "I would have to agree that there doesn't seem to be any other way that her ethylene glycol levels would be high. I'll speak with Barney and the CMO. The hospital has specific protocol for situations like this, and the police will be contacted to investigate. Meanwhile, we'll get started treating her."

A huge breath of relief left her lungs. "Thank you for believing me. For not dismissing the idea because I'm a lowly intern."

A slow smile spread across his face, touched his eyes which grew warm and admiring. He reached out to cup her face in his hands. "Lowly intern? You, Dr. Pappas, are a superstar. Have I told you lately how much you amaze me?"

Without thinking, she pressed her own palm against the back of his hand. "Me, amazing? Not as amazing as you, Dr. Armstrong, surgeon extraordinaire."

A chuckle rumbled in his chest, and their gazes stayed locked on one another's. Memories of their night and day together hummed in the air between them, and both moved forward, their lips meeting for the briefest connection until a voice jolted them apart.

"What...the hell?" Nick was in the hallway, practically right next to where they stood, and Alec's hands fell to his sides as he took a step back. Nick stared then moved in, just inches away. His voice was quiet but filled with a confusion and anger Katy had rarely heard from him. "Are you kidding me?"

Alec's lips were pressed into a thin line, but he regarded Nick steadily. "Katy has come up with an impressive diagnosis for a patient, but wasn't sure anyone would believe her. She came to talk with me about it first."

Nick looked behind them before speaking again in a near whisper. "I may be as dense as my soon-to-be ex-wife claims, but I'm not totally stupid. The excuse you gave for Katy staying with you..." He shook his head, his eyes narrowed. His chest lifted in a deep breath as he glanced down the hallway again. "We'll talk about this later. My office. Tonight."

Katy's stomach churned. How had they let their guard down and allowed themselves even one second of anything smacking of a personal relationship between them while they were here? And a kiss more than smacked of that. It screamed it. Alec's expression had hardened to stone, and her heart sank at the worry and remorse in his eyes.

"Nick, I don't get what you're upset about." Could she play the innocent, clueless Katy and convince him he hadn't seen what he thought he had?

"You—"

"Alec, I need to speak with you."

They all turned to see Barney Boswell walking toward them. His expression was as grim as Nick's, and Katy's heart about stopped. Dear God, had he seen, too? And if so, what would happen?

"Yes?" Alec's voice was even, but his stony expression hadn't changed.

"I've received...bad news." The man rubbed his hand across his face. "My mother has passed away, and I need to help my brother with all the arrangements. I'm leaving in the morning, so you'll have to take over teaching rounds again."

CHAPTER TWELVE

ALEC PACED IN his office, wondering how the hell to handle this latest problem. His gut churned at what a mess it all was—what a mess he'd allowed it to become.

After his magical night and day with Katy he'd wanted more of them. Hadn't wanted it to end. Had convinced himself they could be discreet and completely professional in the hospital. With him no longer doing the teaching rounds, he'd been sure it wouldn't be too difficult to keep their distance by day and be together when their schedules allowed it at night.

That plan had now gone up in flames. How could he possibly justify what had been wrong to begin with if he had to take over the teaching rounds again?

He'd also clearly been kidding himself about their ability to be discreet. After only moments in the hallway with Katy, looking into the intense blue of her eyes as she'd spoken, listening to her impressive detective work on Helen Patterson's illness, he'd forgotten every damned thing except how amazing she was.

He dropped down into his desk chair, wanting to think about all this for a minute before he went to Nick's office, and closed his eyes. They'd been beyond lucky that the only person who'd seen him holding her face in his hands and kissing her had been Nick. And while that brought another dimension into the equation, at least Nick wasn't going to run to the CMO and report a suspicion that a teacher and senior staff member was hitting on a student. Or, at least, he didn't think so, unless Nick thought he'd be protecting his sister if he did.

"So what do you have to say for yourself?"

Alec opened his eyes and saw Nick standing in the doorway, arms folded across his chest, looking almost as angry as he had when he'd first seen them in the hall.

"Do you realize how much you sound like my father right now?"

"Apparently someone damn well has to." Nick came in and perched on the edge of the chair opposite Alec. "I still can't believe what I saw today. How the hell long has this been going on?"

Should he tell him? Or flat-out lie and try to make him believe it had been a friendly, congratulatory kiss?

Alec didn't like either option, but knew he couldn't lie to Nick. "What's going on is that, from the minute I saw Katy again, I haven't been able to stop thinking about her. About her beauty and brains and how damned all-around incredible she is. And, yeah, I knew it was all wrong but couldn't stop it. No matter how hard I tried." He leaned his elbows on his desk and braced himself for the censure he deserved. "When I found out she felt the same way, I couldn't fight it anymore."

"Hell, Alec." Nick stood and paced across the room. "First of all I'm having a hard time wrapping my brain around you and my little sister being…you know…whatever it is you are."

"I know." He couldn't believe it either. But he

didn't have to believe it for his attraction, his obsession with her to have consumed him anyway.

"To think, I was worried people would whisper favoritism because she's my sister. Which thankfully hasn't happened." Nick shook his head. "And I don't even have to say the rest of it, do I? I absolutely can't believe you've done this after all you went through before. You just can't go there. Period. It's bad for you, and it's bad for her. It's just plain bad."

"I know. You think I don't know that?" Alec clenched his fists, wanting to pound on something. "I—"

"It's only bad if you choose to decide it is," a quiet voice said from the doorway.

Both men looked at Katy. Alec's stupid, confused heart felt like it somehow squeezed and swelled at the same time. She stood there in green scrubs that were wrinkled and had some sort of orange stain beneath her breast. Her blue eyes had shadows smudging them and the hair he so loved to touch was pulled back into a messy ponytail that had numerous loose strands sticking out of it…and still she was the most beautiful thing he'd ever seen.

Nick walked over to her. "You two can't do this. A student having a relationship with an attending just isn't done."

"Really? Just isn't done? I've met several couples in this hospital who had exactly that kind of professional relationship before they had a personal one." Her eyes turned to blue steel as she stood toe to toe with Nick, and in spite of the whole damned situation Alec had to smile. This amazing woman standing in front of him was as tough as nails.

"Doesn't make it right. Doesn't make it ethical, and it doesn't mean the hospital won't boot both of you out of here on your asses. You know what happened five years ago when Alec made exactly this same kind of stupid mistake. It blows my mind that he's doing it again. To you, of all people! I won't let you make the same kind of mistake and have your reputation ruined, or worse."

Katy knew what had happened back then? Alec's chest tightened, because he knew everything Nick said was true. Risking her reputation was all kinds of wrong. Except their relationship felt so damned right.

Katy wrapped her arms around her brother's waist and leaned up to kiss him on the cheek. "I keep reminding you I'm a big girl. Alec and I will figure this out, and I promise you—no tears, no matter what."

Nick's face softened slightly as he looked down at his sister. "I love you, Katy, but the last thing you need is to get fired because of misconduct." He turned and pointed his finger at Alec, his eyes fierce. "This is my little sister you're messing with here, and you'd better end this now before she gets hurt."

He stormed out and Alec and Katy were left to just look at one another. Since simply looking at her made him feel alive in a way he hadn't felt in a long time—hell, had never felt—he didn't know what to do.

She took a few steps closer, surprisingly hesitant steps, considering her firm response to her brother a few minutes earlier.

"So, now what?" she asked quietly, her eyes

searching his. "We've both known all along this might happen."

He stood and walked to her, wrapping her in his arms. She laid her head against his chest and he pressed his cheek to her silky hair.

If only there was a solution that would still allow him to hold the softness of her body to his, still tangle his fingers in her hair, still kiss her lush lips whether they were covered with sweet sugar or just savor the sweetness of them alone. A solution where he could enjoy her inquisitive and quirky mind and find ways to make her smile and laugh, which he'd just recently discovered was the best part of any day.

"I didn't know you knew about what happened five years ago," he said.

"I don't know much. Just that you were involved with a teacher of yours when you were a resident, and she ended up getting fired."

Realization dawned. "Is that why you'd been so chilly to me for so long after the wedding when you kissed me? I thought you were just mad about that."

"Hey, wouldn't you be upset, too? I kissed you

and you turned me down flat, saying anything between us wouldn't be appropriate. Then ran right out and had a fling with your teacher just months later. I wanted to hit you." She smiled. "But I know now that's not at all who you are."

"It's who I was then."

"We all learn and grow, don't we?" She stroked his cheek with her hand. "So tell me the whole story."

"I was young and careless. Probably tried to live up to my dad's poor opinion of me." He sighed. "She was only a few years older than I was. But still my teacher and superior. She came on to me and I thought, Why the hell not? Then found out why not."

"What happened?"

"The university and hospital ethics board had a fit. Wanted to boot me out of the residency program." He didn't want to confess the worst part of it, but knew he had to. "My father was furious with me besmirching the Armstrong name that just happens to grace the cardiology wing of that hospital after his revolutionary valve-transplant discovery. He swept my dirty deeds under the rug, while making sure she got fired."

"Did you love her?"

The blue eyes looking up at him had gotten so serious he actually smiled, despite everything. "Hell, no. I barely knew her. From then on I never dated anyone in the hospitals I worked in."

"Then why get involved with me?"

"You're not really asking me that, are you?" He loved the way her brows were drawn together, at the way she seemed to be studying him, trying to figure out what he was thinking. And good luck to her with that, because his mind sure ping-ponged back and forth from moment to moment on how to deal with his feelings and hers and the damned professional risks.

"Yes, I am asking. And you'd better give me an honest answer."

"Because I couldn't resist, Katy-Did. Because I'm crazy about you. So crazy it seemed worth the risk to your reputation and mine too. Even though Nick is right. Risking yours makes me a selfish bastard."

"I knew about your past and the potential consequences but decided I wanted to be with you anyway. And it's still a risk I'm willing to take, if you are."

Her arms tightened around him and squeezed his heart. What should he do here? Could he really walk away from her on the slim chance someone found out and reported it? Could he make himself say goodbye?

His stomach churned, and that sensation made him realize that it wasn't just the thought of damaging her career that had made it feel that way all afternoon. It had been the thought of ending things before they'd even begun to explore what was happening between them.

"I'd never forgive myself if people started talking and it affected your job here."

"I'd never forgive you if you don't let us find out exactly what this is between us."

"I don't think I could stand never being forgiven by you. Having you turn all cold to me the past five years was hard enough." He realized the office door was open a crack, and released her to shove it closed. "I don't know what's right. But I do know that I can't just walk away from you. From this. Without finding out exactly what this is. Even though I know I damn well should." He wrapped his hands around her shoulders and drew her close again, breathing in the scent of her that tormented and teased him whenever she was near.

"Smart man." She smiled, flattening her palms against his chest, warming him. "I was hoping you wouldn't make me turn loose my woman-scorned fury on you."

He chuckled then kissed her cute nose, touched his lips to each soft cheek, to one beautiful eye then the other, before drawing back. "Tomorrow I have to take over teaching rounds again. My having a jones for an intern while being her teacher, supervisor and, in just over a week, giving her an evaluation grade, is completely unethical."

"This is not a news flash, Alec. We—"

"Shh. Let me finish before you unleash the scorned woman on me." He pressed his fingers to her lips, trailed them across her jaw to cup her cheek. "This is a complicated problem I feel requires some special problem-solving skills that a certain beautiful intern I know has in spades."

The irritation in her eyes faded to a smile. "Go on."

"So, I'm borrowing the technique you told me you used to figure out Mrs. Patterson's illness. I defined the goal. And that goal is to put back the sparkle and excitement that's been missing in my life by spending time with you. To kiss every inch of your body until you're in delirious ecstasy, then start all over again. Teach you how to sail, because you nearly got knocked into the water by the boom when we went last time."

"You know I have a clumsiness problem." Her warm hands slid up his chest to rest on each side of his neck. "I like your goals. Except there are three of them, and to truly solve a problem you have to concentrate on one."

"All right. The goal is to add excitement to my life by taking you out on my sailboat and kissing every inch of your body while we're on the water."

She laughed, her eyes now twinkling, and he nearly lost his train of thought while thinking about kissing her delectable body. "Next," he continued, before they never finished the conversation and he ended up making love to her on the floor, "I determined the facts, which is that no one can know about my kissing you all over or anything else that may come to mind."

"I can see you're very good at problem-solving. Did you learn this from my dad, too?" She reached up to nip his lips, nibble, lick, tease. He nearly dove into her mouth to give her a deep kiss and to hell with any and all conversation, but this had to come first.

"No. I learned from you." He kissed her softly, her sweet lips clinging to his. Her fingers slipped from his neck, slid into his hair as she pressed closely against him and he couldn't wait to finish the talking so they could move on to something infinitely more pleasurable.

"Final step is critical thinking." He lifted his hands to her cheeks and looked into the smiling eyes he could lose himself in. "I want you. You want me." Which made him the damned luckiest man on the planet. "We should try being together, not apart. But we have to get through the ten days you're my student being as cold as ice to one another in the hospital."

"That won't be easy for me, since what I'm feeling right now is very, very hot." She pressed her mouth to his chin, his jaw, his throat. "But I'll rise to the challenge."

She always rose to any challenge in front of her. Her mouth on his skin was making his body rise to a challenge, too, and he pulled an inch away before he lost control. "There are still some risks involved. But when you move off of the surgery rotation, it will be fairly easy to be discreet. And if people found out, at that point it would probably result in just a slap on the wrist, nothing more. What do you think?"

"I think your conclusion is most excellent. Just like you."

"Am I allowed to add another goal now?"

"Since you've concluded the last one, you may work on a new one."

He reached behind her and locked the door. "My goal is to enjoy our last few hours together before rounds tomorrow." He tugged her scrub top loose from her drawstring pants and wrapped his hands around her ribs, let them travel upward to cup her breasts, lightly thumbing her nipples.

A pleased gasp left her lips as she arched into him, but touching her wasn't enough. He wanted to see her, too. Moving his hands upward, he grasped her arms to push the cotton fabric up and off her.

"Are you sure no one will walk in?" She covered her breasts with her hands and glanced behind her.

"The door is locked. And this is the private office of a big, bad surgeon. No one will bother me."

"Big, bad surgeon?" She dropped her hands to cover his as they cupped her ribs again. "And here I didn't think you were egotistical."

"Don't be fooled. All surgeons are egotistical." He kissed the top of her breast then slid his mouth across the swell of it to kiss the other. "I love your pretty, lacy bra. And what's inside it. Every time I see you in your scrubs in the hospital, I can't believe how sexy you look in them. Even more now that I know what's under them."

"Scrubs are not sexy. Not on me, anyway. But

on you? Most definitely." Her breathy laugh turned to a low moan as his mouth moved to her nipple beneath the lace. "However, having them off of you is sexier still."

She tugged his shirt over his head, which unfortunately required him to lift his mouth from her. Which he figured was a good opportunity to see more of her skin. All of it. He unclasped her bra and slid it down her arms to the floor. Then tucked his thumbs into her waistband and tugged until she kicked them off her ankles, along with her shoes and socks, yanking off his own clothes in short order.

He paused a moment to just look at her stunning nakedness. At the golden glow of the smooth skin that covered her delectable curves, the sensual smile on her lips, the blue eyes that looked at him with the same desire he felt that nearly overwhelmed him.

Breathless, he tugged her ponytail loose from the band holding it, let her silky hair slide over his hands. Holding her waist in his hands again, he moved backwards, bringing her with him, until he sat in his swivel chair. Let his hands slide to cup the smooth curves of her rear and brought her onto his lap.

"I've never made love in an office before." She straddled him, wrapping her arms around his neck, her hard nipples teasing and tickling his chest. "Is this how it's done?"

"I don't know. I've never made love in an office either. Though I've fantasized about you enough as I sat right here in this chair. And I'm more than excited to have that fantasy become real." He slipped his fingers between her legs, caressing her slick core until she gasped and sighed and pressed against him. She closed her eyes, and the little sounds that came from her beautiful lips made his pulse pound and his breath short. Watching her face as he touched her was beyond erotic, and he nearly plunged inside her that second.

But he didn't. He wanted the moment to last. Wanted to go slow, wanted to hear her sighs, wanted to look into her eyes and the bliss in their blue depths. The scent of her hair and her skin and her arousal nearly drove him mad, and he covered her mouth with his, needing that connection. Needing to taste her sweetness. Needing more of her. The kiss became deep, frenzied, until she lifted herself onto him and they moved together in a primal rhythm. Moved together with a growing need that nearly swamped him.

"Katy." He grasped her hips, trying to slow the moment down, to savor every single second of their joining, but as she tossed her head back, her glorious hair spilling across her shoulders she cried out his name, and he had no choice but to give in to the release, her name on his lips as they fused with hers.

CHAPTER THIRTEEN

THANK HEAVENS TEACHING rounds for the day were almost over, with Mrs. Patterson as their last patient. It was nearly impossible to listen to Alec speak without watching his mouth and remembering all the places on her body it had roamed. To look at his hands as he held a patient's wrist, or touched them in a physical exam without thinking of the places he'd touched her own body and how incredible he'd made her feel. To look at his eyes and remember how they had gazed at her nakedness with a hunger that had set her on fire.

Through sheer force of will she'd managed to make work her number-one focus.

"You look so much better, Helen!" Katy took in the woman's rosy color and bright eyes, and thought she might even have put on a pound or two.

"I certainly feel like a new woman." Helen reached out her hand and Katy clasped it in hers. "Dr. Armstrong here tells me it's all because you figured out what was…going on."

"She did indeed." His expression held warm admiration as he glanced at Katy. "Dr. Pappas is smart and thorough, and we're lucky to have her as an intern here, Mrs. Patterson."

"I know you are." She squeezed Katy's hand. "I want to thank you for saving my life. It's not often someone gets a chance to say that. I know I wasn't far from being on the other side of the grass."

"You don't have to thank me. I'm just glad we were able to figure out what was making you ill." She couldn't imagine how beyond awful it must have made Helen feel to find out Jeffrey was poisoning her, and she didn't want to distress her by bringing it up.

"It's all hard to believe." Her eyes were sad. "A part of me feels bad for my son. That he would be so desperately in debt that he couldn't think of any other way."

Katy didn't reply. It was hard to feel sorry for

someone who would do something so terrible to anyone, let alone his own mother.

"He wasn't trying to kill me, you know." The woman looked at them almost pleadingly, apparently hoping they'd believe her words. "He just thought I'd get sick enough that he'd have my power of attorney. Just long enough to get out of debt, then I'd be okay again. The judge will take into account his gambling problems, I think. I hope he can get over his addiction."

"Addictions are powerful things, Mrs. Patterson, but he's getting the help he needs," Alec said. "Meanwhile, I'd like you to focus on getting back to your old self and walking your dogs again."

Helen smiled. "I can't wait to have them jumping up in my lap. My daughter is bringing them down tomorrow, and I'll be so happy to be home and continuing my physical therapy there." She squeezed Katy's hand tight. "Thank you again, my dear. Oceancrest is very lucky to have you."

"Thank you, Helen. I'll be thinking of you with your pups."

They left the room and Alec paused in the hall

to smile at her. "It's got to make you feel great to see Mrs. Patterson so fit and ready to go home. Congratulations."

"Thank you."

"I hope you both remember this." Alec turned to Todd Eiterman and Michael Coffman. "Sometimes you have to look for the zebra when the first answer doesn't seem to make sense. I'll see you for rounds tomorrow."

He strode down the hall without a backward glance, with Todd following, and she quickly turned her attention to her schedule as she pulled it from her pocket.

"Must be nice to be teacher's pet," Michael said. His tone of voice was light but his expression wasn't.

"I'm not teacher's pet." Her stomach constricted a little, even though she knew he couldn't mean it in a personal way. "I just got lucky with the diagnosis, and I'm sure you will too some time."

"Yeah. I can only hope," he said. "Got more scut work to do. See you later."

She breathed a deep sigh of relief. Had she and

Alec actually managed to always keep poker faces around one another the past week? Had not a single person noticed how their eyes sometimes met and clung, before they both quickly looked away? She hoped and prayed no one had. Thank heavens they wouldn't have to be under such a strain much longer.

Only four more days. Four more days of the stress of hiding how she felt about him while they rounded together. Though they'd still have to be discreet at the hospital when they did run into one another.

A smile spread across her face, and she hoped no one noticed that either. Because she knew it was a silly, lust-struck kind of smile that came every time she thought of their forced separation being over with. A smile from wondering what kind of quiet, behind-the-scenes relationship might blossom between them.

She shook her head to dispel all thoughts of Alec so she could concentrate on the work in front of her. Her next assignment was to give conscious sedation to a patient who required a special IV line that would be inserted into his neck vein. Just a few weeks ago she might have been a nervous wreck about doing it, and she felt a little proud at how far she'd come in such a short time.

Katy looked at the chart in her hand. Room 4280. Patient Richard Wynne. Elizabeth would be there to supervise as Katy performed the procedure.

She knocked on the doorjamb of the surgical intensive care room, then stepped inside with a smile. "Mr. Wynne? I'm Dr. Pappas. I'm here to insert the central IV line you need."

The man grimaced. "Sounds like it might hurt like hell."

"Don't worry." She came close and gave him what she hoped was a reassuring smile. "We'll be giving you an intravenous drug to make you drowsy. Technically, you'll be awake but you won't remember anything."

"I'll be awake but won't remember it afterward?"

"Strange, huh? But that's the way it works." She'd learned that patients didn't really have to know the details of how retrograde amnesia drugs worked, only that they did. She'd also learned not to tell patients she was a newbie at these procedures, unless they asked. Usually, they freaked out, and who could blame them? "I'll be assisted by Dr. Stark."

He nodded, seemingly satisfied. Katy cleaned up and put on a gown, mask, and gloves. The nurse brought all the necessary equipment, and Katy prepped the man's skin by sponging on a sterile soap solution. She and the nurse got the man draped to create a sterile field, his neck exposed by a hole in the fabric, and again Katy felt pretty darned proud how competent she'd become at all of it.

All systems go, she thought with satisfaction. She and the nurse sat there waiting quietly, Katy looking at her watch every few minutes. Where was Elizabeth? She should have been here twenty minutes ago. Katy tried calling her but got no answer.

"Is there some problem?" Mr. Wynne asked with a frown.

"I'm sorry, I'm not sure what the delay is." The man looked quite annoyed, which Katy could well understand. All draped and having to stay motionless, ready to get it over with, then lying there endlessly waiting. "Dr. Stark should be here any moment. I'll see if I can find her."

Katy looked up and down the hall, but there was no sign of Elizabeth. What should she do here?

"Something wrong, Dr. Pappas?"

Alec's deep voice seemed to rumble right into her chest, and her heart leaped as she looked up at him. His expression was carefully neutral as his eyes met hers, and she quickly schooled her own to look the same.

"As you likely recall, this patient is having extensive bowel surgery tomorrow, and we couldn't get a line placed in his arm. So I'm here to insert a central venous catheter in his neck, and Dr. Stark is supposed to supervise me. But she's not here and I can't find her."

Alec frowned and glanced into the room. "Obviously you have the patient ready. I assume you haven't given him sedation yet?"

"Not yet. I was waiting for Elizabeth."

"We need to just get this done. I'll supervise you."

Katy's heart did a little pit-pat in her chest as they walked together into the small room. She was all too aware of him as he stood just an inch away. Aware of the warmth of his body in the chilly room. Aware of his distinctive scent. Aware of his eyes lingering on her before turning to the patient.

She sucked in a breath and focused her attention on the procedure she had to perform, her hands sweating a little inside her gloves. Why did she suddenly feel so nervous about him watching her do this? She knew the answer. She was afraid she just might not do as good a job as he would expect her to, and she so wanted him to be impressed. Maybe that was vain and shallow, when she should be most concerned about the patient, but couldn't help the feeling.

She reminded herself she was a professional and needed to think and act like one. Not a nervous nellie newbie who had to cut into someone's skin in just a few minutes.

Alec moved a short distance away to scrub,

gown, and mask himself before he came to stand beside her again. "Go ahead, Dr. Pappas. I'm here to assist you with anything you need," Alec said. Katy glanced up at him and while his face was mostly obscured by the mask, she could see the small smile in his eyes, see him give her a little encouraging nod, which instantly helped her relax.

"Okay." She stopped short of saying, *Here goes nothing*, figuring the patient wouldn't exactly be reassured by that. She drew the sedation into the syringe and injected it smoothly into Mr. Wynne's arm. Within seconds his eyelids drooped and it was obvious he was already under its effect. No matter how many times she saw it used, the speed with which the drug worked always amazed her.

The nurse handed her the small knife and Katy looked up at Alec, who gifted her with another smile from his eyes and another nod. Steeling herself, she turned to make the tiny incision in the man's neck. When she was finished, she carefully slid the central line, half the width of a pencil, through the skin and down into the patient's jugular vein.

When it was finally done, Katy realized she'd been holding her breath, and let it out in a whoosh. "All done, I think. Did I do okay?"

"Better than okay. You did great."

Alec's eyes now weren't just smiling, they were crinkled at the corners like she loved to see, and she grinned back. "Are you sure you don't want to be a surgeon?" he asked. "It just might be your calling after all."

"No thanks. But I do admit I've loved being on this service and learning all this cool stuff. Thanks for being a wonderful teacher."

"Thanks for being a wonderful student." He placed his palm between her shoulder blades and gave her a quick pat before he turned to take off his mask and gown.

"Excuse me, Dr. Armstrong."

Both Alec and Katy turned to see Elizabeth standing there. A very angry Elizabeth, whose fists were clenched and lips were pressed together into a thin line. Katy's heart flipped in alarm at her expression. Then reminded herself nothing inappropriate had happened. Alec had just given her the same kind of congratulatory shoulder pat she'd seen him give to all the interns and residents.

"Yes, Dr. Stark?" Alec's expression was cool, neutral, but Katy didn't think she was imagining the wariness in his eyes.

"With all due respect, sir, it was my job to supervise Dr. Pappas for this procedure. Why are you doing it?"

"Because you weren't here, and the patient had been ready for some time." Alec's voice was firm and authoritative. "When Dr. Pappas told me she'd been unable to locate you, I decided to supervise. There's no reason to keep a patient waiting unnecessarily when another physician gets delayed, is there?"

"My delay was unavoidable. Dr. Pappas should have waited for me instead of soliciting you to do my job."

"It was actually I who volunteered to supervise when I realized you'd been delayed." Alec regarded Elizabeth steadily, seemingly not affected by her surprising anger. "At no time did

I think you not being here reflects on the quality of your work or your reliability, Dr. Stark, if that's what's worrying you. If you'd like to talk about this further, please come to my office later. Meanwhile, you may finish up with Dr. Pappas."

Without a backward glance Alec moved past Elizabeth and left the room.

With Alec gone, Elizabeth glanced at the nurse then turned to Katy. "May I speak with you privately?"

Katy trailed after her into the hallway, dismayed when Elizabeth turned and pointed her finger at her. "You. What a gunner you are." The resident's voice was shaking. "Always trying to make yourself look good and to hell with anybody else looking bad because of it."

"I don't know what you mean." Katy's stomach knotted. "I've just tried to learn and do my work on this rotation."

"That is such a load of bull. Every time I turn around you're talking to Dr. Armstrong about this or that, asking questions, trying to sound so smart. Trying to make everyone else look stupid. I wouldn't be surprised if you tried to get into Alec's pants just to win points from an attending. Don't think I haven't noticed the way you flirt with him. The way he looks at you."

Katy gasped and felt all the blood drain from her face. Had Elizabeth really noticed the vibe between them? Surely this must just be her lashing out at her because the woman put so much pressure on herself to succeed in a man's world.

"Elizabeth, I hope you don't really believe that of me. That I was trying to build myself up by putting other people down. And I'm certain Dr. Armstrong views me only as an intern who needs all the help I can get. I've seen how hard you work and what a good surgeon you are. I know it's tough to be a female surgeon, and I honestly wish the best for you."

To Katy's shock, Elizabeth's eyes filled with tears before she turned away. "Head on to your next assignment, please, and I'll finish with Mr. Wynne."

Should she try to talk out this shocking hostility from Elizabeth a little more? As she watched the woman remove Mr. Wynne's drape, she decided she'd leave it for now. Perhaps it was a conversation better suited to the tavern.

She headed to the next floor to see a patient, a cold chill running down her spine as she recalled Elizabeth's ugly words about trying to get into Alec's pants to win points and noticing the way he looked at her. Would Elizabeth ever suggest to someone else that Katy might have done that?

The chill spread to every inch of her body when she thought of the ugly turn gossip like that could take if her relationship with Alec became public.

"Thanks, everybody, for staying late and for doing such a great job. As always, you make Oceancrest one of the best hospitals around," Alec said to the medical staff as he finished his last surgery of one damned long day.

"Dr. Armstrong, can I speak with you real quickly? Privately?" a nurse asked.

"Of course." Alec stripped off his gloves and walked out of the OR to the empty hallway, with the nurse following. "What's on your mind?"

"I really respect you, so I wanted you to know there's some talk going around."

His heart practically stopped before it sped up into a fast rhythm. "Talk?"

She leaned closer. "One of the residents was talking about Dr. Pappas being your favorite, and implying some things I'm sure you don't want implied."

"What kind of things?"

"Like she gets more attention from you because she's Nick Pappas's sister. Even worse, that she's been coming on to you to get a good evaluation."

Holy hell. His breath backed up into his lungs. "Is this…rumor all over the hospital, or confined to just a few people on the surgical service?"

"I don't really know. I've only heard it around surgery, but that's where I hang out most of the time. Anyway, I thought you'd want to know."

"Thank you. I do want to know. And for what it's worth, Dr. Pappas is a very upstanding intern, and my evaluation of her will be strictly professional."

She nodded. "Of course I know that, Dr. Armstrong. You're one of the most professional doctors at this hospital."

His chest compressed even tighter at her words. He moved on to the locker room and stripped out of his scrubs, feeling a little numb. His mind spun back to his interactions with Katy, and other than that brief kiss in the hallway that Nick had seen couldn't think of anything that would start the rumor mill going.

Except that he knew, damn it, the way he looked at her sometimes. Had caught himself giving her goo-goo eyes on a few occasions, but hadn't thought anyone had seen.

He could only hope and pray that the gossip was minor. Wasn't juicy enough to spread through the hospital or garner much interest. How could it be? From what the nurse had said, it was a minor comment that probably stemmed from jealousy at what a great job Katy was doing and nothing more.

Trying to relax his tense muscles and tamp down the nag of anxiety, Alec got dressed, glad the long day was over. Glad that what had seemed like the longest week ever was almost over. Just a few more days with the stress and pressure of being sure he didn't look at Katy or talk to her or smile at her in any way that might be misconstrued by observers.

Misconstrued? That was the crux of it, because there would be no misinterpretation to think his looks and smiles came from his all-too-vivid memories of making love with her, and thoughts of how he wanted more of it. More of her.

A nasty niggle of worry over this whole situation stayed stuck in his gut. A different, crappy feeling would definitely lodge there instead, though, if they decided the risk to both their careers was too big.

He picked up his shirt, realizing her addictive scent lingered on it. Realized it was the shirt he'd been wearing when they'd last made love. He lifted it to his nose and inhaled, and just that tiny memory of her stepped up his pulse and shortened his breath.

What a damned complicated situation. But surely they could keep their cool around one another for just a few more days until she was off the surgical rotation. After that the chances were good they'd barely see one another in the hospital and any germs of gossip would quickly die.

He'd call her to tell her what the nurse had said then double his efforts to keep his feelings hidden while they were at work.

CHAPTER FOURTEEN

"How much do you think they're paying this guy?" Nick whispered, leaning toward Alec. "I could put together a better lecture than this."

"Maybe. But then you'd alienate everyone in the room, because you wouldn't be able to resist throwing in a few opinions about how certain specialists are usually prima donnas."

"True." Nick chuckled, turning his attention back to the lectern.

The county-wide hospital meeting had been going on for hours, and Alec was glad this was the last speaker before lunch was served. Though, among the duds, there were always interesting presentations on new research and updates specific to general surgery and other surgical specialties. At their table sat doctors from three other medical centers, and it was always good to catch up with them, too.

Alec tried his best to not look across the room where Katy sat with other residents and interns, and was pleased he managed to accomplish that. Most of the time, anyway, until he occasionally caught his gaze sliding her way.

Apparently, he wasn't the only one ready for lunch as chatter broke out instantly when the presentation ended and food was served. He found himself wondering if Katy had ordered the fish or the chicken then shook his head at himself. Why the hell would that even cross his mind? The answer clearly was that she was on his mind, period, even when the subject was inane.

"Her name is Pappas," he heard a voice say at the next table, and he and Nick both paused their eating and turned their heads at the same time as the name caught their ears. A man was pointing across the room toward Katy's table. "I can't remember her first name."

"Kathy, maybe?" another voice said, then chuckled as he looked across the room in Katy's direction. "Yeah, I heard the same thing about her. But there are always a few of them, you know. She's pretty enough to tempt any attending into thinking with the wrong head."

He stared at Nick who stared back at him, and his heart thumped hard as an ice-cold chill swept through him. What the hell were they saying about Katy?

"Doesn't the CMO know what's going on?"

"I hear she's got all the docs wrapped around her little finger. Or maybe it's because she's got her legs wrapped around them," someone said, eliciting chuckles.

"She's the kind of doctor that gives the rest of us a bad name," a woman said. "Most of us don't have to sleep around to get a good evaluation. Though I admit there was one resident I knew who slept with every attending she worked with."

A man chuckled. "And what I want to know is why I wasn't ever lucky enough to have a female student like that."

As the entire table laughed, Alec had trouble swallowing the bite of food he'd stuck in his mouth when they'd first heard the chatter. After he got it down, it sat in his stomach like lead and he had trouble catching his breath.

He turned to look at Nick, who stared right back at him. Nick's eyes were hard, his lips pressed tightly together, but he didn't say a word.

He didn't have to. Alec knew what Nick was thinking, and knew he was right. He also knew what had to happen next. And it had to happen in a way Katy couldn't argue with.

It was late in the afternoon when Katy made her way toward where she, Alec and Nick had arranged to meet up after the day conference. While the presentations had been interesting, she was more than glad it was over. After checking a few patients, she'd get to go home, put her feet up and have a leisurely evening with Nick and hopefully Alec, too.

Since her brother had been so disapproving of anything smacking of a relationship between her and Alec, the two of them had agreed to stay just friendly around each other while Nick was around. To let some time go by until she'd been off his teaching service for quite a while.

Maybe by then Nick would see their relationship was important to both of them and that, hopefully, at that point it wouldn't jeopardize either of their careers.

She made her way through the crowd of people then headed out to the parking lot, spotting Nick next to the car, along with some woman. Alec was there, too, and seeing his smile made her heart swell. Quickly, she tamped it down, knowing her feelings would be written all over her face if she didn't.

Then realized Alec had his arm wrapped around the woman's shoulders. A very pretty woman, and his hold seemed more intimate than friendly. Her steps slowed as she stared then stopped completely as his arm slipped to the woman's waist, tightened around her to draw her close. His handsome head dipped down and he kissed the woman on the cheek.

Then moved on to her mouth, lingering. Their lips separated an inch and held that position, almost nose to nose, before he pressed his lips to the woman's again for a long, long moment as she raised her palm to his face.

Katy felt like she couldn't breathe. What in the world...? Surely this wasn't what it looked like. It couldn't be.

She forced herself to start moving again, reassuring herself this had to be just a friend of his or something. But her gut knew that no two people who were just friends kissed the way she'd just seen them kiss.

As she approached them she was sure Alec would drop his arm from the woman's waist, but he didn't. Numbness began to seep through her body when she stopped to stand next to Nick.

"Hey, Katy," Alec said, smiling at her. Smiling as though there was nothing strange about his holding another woman close when he'd made love to Katy just days ago. "Did you learn a lot from the presentations?"

"Yes. They were interesting." She managed to say the words through a throat so tight it hurt. "Aren't you going to introduce me to your... friend?"

"Oh, sorry. This is Andrea Walton. She and I, and Nick too, were residents together." To Katy's disbelief, he actually gave the woman another lingering kiss on her forehead. "I didn't know she was working at Holland Memorial now, and was pretty excited to see her here today. Andrea, this is Nick's little sister, Katy."

Nick's little sister. Pretty excited to see Andrea. Katy felt woozy, but told herself she was making a mountain out of a molehill. Maybe Alec held and kissed all old friends who were female.

"It's nice to meet you, Katy. I hear you're an intern. Alec tells me you're a good student," Andrea said.

"Nice to meet you, too."

"Hey, listen," Alec said, "Andrea and I are going to head out and get some dinner before I take her sailing. Just like old times." Alec smiled at Andrea and damned if he didn't give her another kiss on the mouth right in front of Katy.

Suddenly, her numbness and shock began to give way to anger. Alec was going to give her an explanation for all this, and what it did or didn't mean, and he was going to do it right now.

"Can I speak with you privately for a second, Alec?"

"Sure." He finally dropped his arm from curving around Andrea and followed Katy a few yards away.

She turned to him, and didn't know what to think of the expression of apology and guilt on his face. "What's going on here? Who is Andrea?"

"I told you, she and I were residents together. She was also my girlfriend for awhile, as you probably figured out."

"Yeah, since I have that analytical brain and all." Her voice shook and she swallowed to control it. "Not that it would have been hard for anyone to figure out since you were kissing her right here in public."

"I was pretty crazy about her, but she got a job all the way across the country." He gave her a crooked, apologetic smile. "Listen, I know you're not going to like this. But, well, seeing her made me realize I never really got over her. And I want to see if we can have what we had before."

Katy swayed a little on her feet, unable to

breathe. Was this really happening? "You want to date her."

"I do." He leaned closer, speaking low. "I'm sorry, but it was never a good idea for us to be involved to begin with, you know that. It's not good for your career, and I frankly don't want to risk my reputation again. I'm sure you understand. Andrea is my peer, which makes her perfect for me."

Perfect for him. "Alec, surely you don't mean this." The words were out of her mouth before she realized she was dangerously close to begging him to stay with her. And she'd never do that with any man.

"It's best for both of us, Katy. You know, you look a little tired." Alec patted her on the head and smiled like he was her uncle or something. "Why don't you go to bed early and get some sleep?"

While he took Andrea to dinner and out on his boat and made love with the woman, just like he'd done with her.

She didn't know how to respond to his words without screaming at him and beating him with her fists like she wanted to. Tears threatened to choke her, and she dragged in a shaky, shocked breath before turning away.

He stopped her with a hand on her shoulder then ran his finger from her forehead to her nose. "I hope we can still be friends."

Friends? Was he kidding? When he'd given her the brush-off long ago she'd been hurt. What she was feeling now after being foolish enough to sleep with a man with his kind of history was so far beyond hurt it was off the charts. "Thanks for the offer, but I don't want to be friends with you."

Somehow she managed to turn and get into the car before the tears began to fall.

CHAPTER FIFTEEN

KATY HAD BEEN too stunned to speak as she and Nick had driven back to the hospital to check on patients before they went home. Too busy swallowing back the tears and trying to wrap her brain around what had just happened.

As she talked with her patients and did her work, she felt like an automaton. Going through the motions in a state of utter numbness. Even when they grabbed a carryout dinner to take home she didn't speak about it to Nick. Didn't know what to say.

By the next morning, though, her disbelief had morphed into an anger so intense, so deep she had to let some of it spill out. Had to get some answers. When she and Nick walked into the hospital together, she turned to him and spoke.

"Can you explain to me what happened yesterday?"

"I assume you're talking about Alec?" Nick's expression was grim. "No. But I can't say I'm sorry, Katy. I am sorry that you feel hurt. But Alec was never right for you anyway."

And wasn't that an understatement? Still, she needed some explanation for how one minute Alec had been making love with her and the next he was kissing another woman. Except, oh, wait. That's the kind of man he was.

"Did he date that woman a long time when you all were residents? Was he...crazy in love with her or something?" Just the question made her chest hurt.

"They were close, I guess." His tone was strangely stiff and he wrapped his arm around her shoulders in a quick hug. "Listen, I know you feel bad right now. But it's for the best."

"Obviously." Her voice shook. "But you're the one who told me he wasn't the kind of guy I thought he was. A player. Why would you say that when you've known him forever? When you know exactly what he's really like?"

"He's my friend, regardless." Nick sighed. "I've got surgery scheduled and need to get to work. We can talk about this later but, honestly, I don't know what else there is to say."

She watched him head down the hallway, and fought back tears yet again. Then she squared her shoulders. She would not allow jerk-of-the-decade Alec to ruin even one day of her life. Somehow, some way, she'd have to get through rounding with him a couple more days. How, exactly, she didn't know. But she would not let him think for even one minute she was heartbroken.

Though at the moment that organ felt crushed into a million little pieces inside her chest.

She forced herself to march down the hall to meet the crew for morning rounds. When she saw Alec standing there talking to Elizabeth and Todd, her confidence wavered and a horrible feeling swept through her body. A peculiar tornado of fury and grief and humiliation, and the sensation was so overwhelming it was all she could do to keep going.

His eyes met hers for only the briefest moment before he turned away. Her throat closed at how gorgeous he looked on the outside. How could he have turned out to be so shallow on the inside? She wanted to scream at him but shoved her anger and pain down as best she could.

Becoming a good doctor was tremendously important to her. She couldn't believe she'd allowed herself to fall for him, especially after trying so hard to remain true to her goal of becoming a respected, admired doctor. The kind of doctor her father would have been proud of. From this moment on she'd give every ounce of her heart to her work.

"Congratulations on a great job today and all month long," Alec said to the young doctors standing with him, beyond thankful the last day of surgical teaching rounds was over with.

He'd known it would be difficult to work with Katy for a few more days after the scene he'd orchestrated with Andrea. But he hadn't begun to realize the depth of that difficulty.

It had been torture. Torture to look into her beautiful eyes and see only ice blue staring back at him. Torture to hear the disgust for him in her voice when she spoke. Torture to be close to her, to have her scent wrap around him, to want to touch the silkiness of her hair and skin and know he'd never again have that pleasure.

He thought it had been disturbing when she'd been chilly to him the past few years? That had been nothing compared to the deep freeze he knew she'd feel toward him forever, and had to wonder if what he'd done had been a terrible mistake.

"I'll be finishing your evaluations and turning them in to Dr. Sanders, who will give them to you this evening. Best of luck to all of you." One by one, he shook their hands. When he got to Katy's it felt as cold as the eyes that stared at him but still he didn't want to let it go.

He didn't have to. Katy yanked it from his after only the briefest shake and turned away. He watched her walk down the hall with the others. Watched the slight sway of her hips, watched her lustrous hair swish across her shoulders.

Watched her walk out of his life.

With a painful hollow in his chest he went to his office to somehow work on the evaluations. But the papers kept blurring into images of Katy.

He knew he'd hurt her badly. Hearing those

people saying such ugly things about her had sent him into protective overdrive, but he realized now that maybe he hadn't thought it through well enough.

Andrea had been his friend for years. She'd been around during the nasty scandal in his past, and had been nice enough to go along with his ploy to end it with Katy because she knew what it had been like for him. Katy had stubbornly insisted she wasn't worried about the risks to her reputation, and wouldn't have accepted it then either, he knew.

But had handling it that way been the right decision? Alec leaned back in his office chair and closed his eyes. At this point he supposed it didn't matter. It was over and done with.

Over and done with. Just like his relationship with Katy.

"Katy," he said out loud, just wanting to hear her name. She was smart and beautiful and wonderful and would be an incredible family practice doc someday, and he could not be the cause of others besmirching her name. No matter how much it hurt, and it hurt beyond anything he'd ever experienced, he'd stay away from her. For her sake, and for the sake of her future.

Hurting *her* that way, though, stabbed like a knife so deeply in his own heart he could barely stand the pain. He hoped she'd get over it soon and move on to someone else who wasn't her superior in the hospital. That thought twisted the knife even deeper, but he'd somehow endure it for her.

A knock on his door had him opening his eyes. "Come in."

Nick appeared and sat in the chair opposite, slumping back into it much like Alec was slumped in his. He had a thick sheaf of papers in his hands. "Guess what arrived today."

"What?"

"My divorce papers from my beloved wife's attorney." His voice was both bitter and pained. "I guess this is really happening."

"You thought it might not?"

"I hadn't admitted it even to myself. But getting these made me realize I thought it wouldn't. I thought maybe she'd change her mind."

"I'm sorry, Nick." What else was there to say?

"Me, too." His lips twisted as he looked at Alec. "We're two pretty pathetic jerks, aren't we?"

"Yeah." He was pathetic and most definitely a jerk.

"I'm going to say something, and you're going to be shocked as hell by it."

Alec raised his eyebrows. "Is this going to be some deep confession about your marriage or your private life? I'm not sure I want to know."

"No. But it's my nearly over marriage that's made me decide to say it." With his elbows on his knees, Nick leaned forward. "I was upset as hell about you and Katy, and even more upset when I heard those people talking about her. But seeing how sad and hurt she is now is upsetting me in a different way."

"Breakups hurt, Nick, as you well know. But we all eventually get over it and move on. Katy will, and you will, too." Though he wasn't too sure about himself.

"I do know. But I also know that sometimes when you really love someone you have to be willing to make a sacrifice. I wasn't willing to sacrifice what I thought was most important, which was my job at Oceancrest, and never mind that I worked so much it was one of the things that killed my marriage." He looked Alec in the eye. "Do you love my sister?"

Alec hadn't thought about putting his feelings into words. But as he sat there, nearly overwhelmed by the awful emptiness in his chest, he knew he did. "Yes. But it doesn't matter."

"It's the only thing that matters. That's what these papers made me realize today." He held them up. "It's probably too late to get Meredith back. But I am going to do something that, if I ever have a chance to fix things, will go a long way to help make that happen."

"I hope it's not that you're going to bomb the company that talked her into moving to New York."

"No." Nick gave him a glimmer of a smile. "I'm going to leave Oceancrest and start a private surgical practice so I can be in control of how many hours I work. And I'd like you to consider joining me."

A private surgical practice? Alec knew that usually meant more flexibility with the work schedule, and sometimes even more money, but he hadn't considered doing anything like that so early in his career. He'd been convinced he needed to establish the respect of everyone in the medical community first. Earn his father's respect first. "That alone would take a huge amount of time and effort to get going."

"I know. But then I'd be in charge of my own destiny. For a lot of reasons I've realized I want that." He stood up. "Think about it. And while you're doing that, think about one more thing. Which is that you love Katy and I know she loves you. I hate to see you both miserable the way I am about Meredith. If you join me, you'll be out of Oceancrest. Ethical problem solved."

Alec sat up straighter. Could that work? And would Katy ever forgive him for lying to her?

It was time to do some thinking. And the best place to do that was in the middle of Mission Bay.

CHAPTER SIXTEEN

KATY HAD NEVER been a person who wanted to drown her sorrows in alcohol, but she was about to make tonight the exception.

The residents and interns were extra-happy at the tavern happy hour, celebrating the end of the month's rounds before they moved on to the next rotation. Most were beaming at the good evaluations they'd received, though a few looked a little glum over their drinks. Katy felt more than glum, and never mind that Alec had given her the highest evaluation possible.

She should be proud and happy. Instead, she just felt relieved that she wouldn't have to work with Alec again. Wouldn't have to look at his amber eyes and handsome face and sexy body and picture him with Andrea, which made her feel so angry she wanted to hit something, and so hurt it gouged all the way to her soul.

She had to get over it. She'd known he was a player. A man who did as he pleased and twisted the rules to suit himself. Then she'd promptly forgotten all that when he'd kissed her. She'd let him wiggle inside her heart just like the worm he was until he'd dumped her like a hot potato when he'd tired of her.

She took a swig of her margarita to swallow down the bitterness filling her chest.

"What are you looking so mad about?" Elizabeth asked as she sat down beside her. "I am absolutely sure Dr. Armstrong gave you a great evaluation."

"Why are you so sure?" Probably because she thought what she'd said before. That Katy had dived into Alec's pants for good marks, and, boy, did she regret diving into them for a whole different reason.

"Honestly?" Elizabeth regarded her steadily. "Because you are one of the best interns I've ever worked with."

Katy stared at her in surprise. "Thank you. That's...nice of you to say."

"It's just the truth," Elizabeth said. "And I have

another truth. A true confession about something I'm not proud of. Something you need to know."

Katy looked at her, wondering what she could be talking about.

"I was jealous of the way Alec looked at you, then it became pretty obvious there was something between you two. I think he's hot, but he never looked twice at me. I'm ashamed to admit this now but I said something to a couple other residents. Next thing I knew, a bunch of people were talking about you sleeping with him."

Katy gasped. "Are you kidding?"

"I wish I was." Elizabeth's lips twisted. "It's my fault, but I swear I never meant it to go any further than my few friends. I'm really sorry. Honest."

She looked at Elizabeth and realized she was telling the truth. That she did feel bad about it, and Katy had made enough mistakes in her own life that she wasn't going to judge Elizabeth too harshly for it. After all, it didn't really matter any more anyway. Alec had moved on.

"Thank you for telling me. Hopefully any

more talk will die off since I won't be around him now."

"Won't you be? Anyone paying attention could tell he's crazy about you."

"No, he's not. He's got a girlfriend."

Elizabeth stared at her. "You're not his girlfriend?"

"Nope."

"You're just saying that because you're not supposed to be involved with an attending. Believe me, I was more than willing to be involved with him, and to heck with the rules." Elizabeth smiled. "I swear I'll never gossip about you again. But I have to tell you. I saw him kissing you in the hall."

Ah, damn. But again, it didn't really matter. But since Elizabeth knew, for some pathetic reason Katy wanted to unload on her. Maybe she'd feel better talking to another woman about it all.

"Okay. I thought we were involved. But when we were at the hospital meeting at the hotel he told me he didn't want to see me any more because he'd run into an old flame named Andrea Walton he hadn't known was in town." Just saying the woman's name made her stomach cramp. "She must work at a different hospital. And he kissed her right in front of me. The jerk."

To her surprise, Elizabeth burst out laughing. "Andrea Walton worked here for a while, so I can tell you she's not new to town. She's also married to a hunky cardiologist who happens to be a partner in her practice, and they have two cute little kids. I guarantee you they are not seeing one another. At least, not in a romantic sense."

Katy stared at her. Was there any way what she said could be true? And if so, why would Alec lie about it?

"I want to make it up to you for being catty and starting tongues wagging, so here's my advice," Elizabeth said, leaning in. "Ask Alec why he would lie to you, because he obviously did. I wouldn't be surprised if he heard the gossip about you and couldn't stand being the reason for it. If I were you, and I frankly wish I was, I'd be his girlfriend no matter what the hospital policy was on that. Go for it, girl."

Alec *had* been worried about her reputation

and about any gossip. Was it at all possible that was why he'd broken up with her?

Maybe it wasn't. Maybe he really had moved on. But it was worth risking one more bash to her heart to find out for sure.

"Thanks, Elizabeth." Katy shoved her drink aside, grabbed her purse and headed out the door. Twenty minutes later she was pulling her car into the parking lot outside Alec's condo, her heart thumping nervously. What if Elizabeth was completely wrong? What if she banged on Alec's door and a half-naked Andrea opened it?

She gulped, but got out of the car anyway. She knew he'd still been at work just an hour ago, and did the math. Even if he'd left the second she'd been given her evaluation, which was unlikely, he would have gotten home only a short time ago.

In any case, she reminded herself sternly, whatever happened this evening would be good. If she found a naked Andrea there, she'd have that answer. If it was just Alec, she'd pay more careful attention to his expression and the tone of his voice if he rejected her again. After all, she'd known him most of her life and could read him pretty well. Or thought she could. Which brought her full circle to thinking she didn't really know him at all.

She shook her head at herself then squared her shoulders, about to head to his front door. Out of the corner of her eye she saw a distinctive sail coming from the center of the bay toward shore. The sail of Alec's boat, which was white with a cobalt-blue triangle in the top corner.

Lord, please do not have Andrea sailing with him and kissing him, she prayed. Going through that again would be beyond torture.

She pulled off her shoes and walked along the sand toward the dock, reaching it just as he smoothly slid the boat in. Her heart pounding so loud in her ears it nearly drowned out the sound of the surf, Katy stepped onto the planks of the dock. Alec stood on the boat, his tanned arms reaching to tie a line to the dock post.

Her heart stuttered at how gorgeous he looked with his muscular legs wide apart on the rocking boat, his hair tossing in the wind, his chiseled features covered only slightly by his sunglasses.

At least they could have this conversation alone, she thought as a breath of relief left her chest.

He looked up at her, and his hands and arms stilled in the middle of tying the line. She wished she could see the expression in his eyes behind the lenses of the sunglasses but had no idea what he was thinking. Hopefully it wasn't horror that she'd shown up on his doorstep.

"I'd like to talk to you, Alec," she said, summoning every ounce of bravery she could muster.

Without saying a word, he finished tethering the line and reached his hand out to her. She grasped it in hers and stepped onto the boat's deck.

Now that she was there, she felt utterly paralyzed. What, exactly, should she say? Have you had sex with Andrea yet? Were you being truthful, or were you lying? I love you, please don't leave me.

And wouldn't the last be beyond pathetic? But standing so close to him now, holding his hand and staring up at him, the words nearly fell from her mouth anyway, and she swallowed.

"I'm glad I found you here. I need to know if you really are involved with Andrea. I need to know if you really don't care for me. That you don't want to be with me. I want the truth."

Her chest felt both heavier and lighter now that she'd asked. Relieved that she'd managed to get the words out but scared to death to hear his response.

"The truth?" Alec took off his sunglasses, and the deep seriousness of his eyes closed her throat. "The truth is I'm an idiot."

"Right now, I can't disagree."

"I don't blame you." He nodded. "What would you say if I told you I lied to you? That I never had anything with Andrea, not in the past and sure as hell not today."

The giant weight on her chest lifted a little, but at the same time her lungs burned with anger. "I'd say you are a giant jerk to hurt me so badly. To make me suffer the way I've been suffering. Then I'd ask you why you lied."

"Ah, Katy." He dropped her hand, shoving his own through his hair. "I'm so sorry I lied. I'm sorry I made you suffer. If it means anything, I can tell you I'm pretty sure I've suffered even more than you."

The anger burned even hotter in her chest, realizing that he'd set up the whole scene with Andrea intentionally to hurt her and drive her away. Yet with the anger came hope that what he said next could bring them close again, instead of driving an even deeper and permanent wedge between them. "Why would you lie and tell me such a horrible thing if it wasn't true?"

"Because people had started to talk and say nasty things about you. I couldn't bear it. And my being the cause of it was even more unbearable." He lifted her chin with his hand to look into her eyes. "I knew if I told you we couldn't be together for that reason, you'd say it didn't matter. But it did matter, Katy. It mattered to me that people were telling ugly lies that could damage what should be a stellar reputation for a stellar intern. It mattered to me that it was my fault."

"And so you, almighty surgeon Alec Armstrong, thought you should play God and decide what's best for me? Lie to me and break my heart, all in the name of what's 'good' for me? I'm more than capable of deciding what's good for me. I can make my own decisions regarding my life and my future."

"I know. I'm sorry. I know I was wrong to lie to you in such a terrible way. It seemed like the best thing at the time, but since then I've thought about what that must have felt like. How much it would have destroyed me to have you do something like that to me. All I can do is tell you I'm sorry and beg you to forgive me. Will you?"

"I don't know. Give me a reason to forgive you."

"You want a reason?" He cupped her cheek in his hand then lowered his lips to hers in a soft, tender kiss. "I don't have a good enough reason for what I did. The only reason I can offer in asking for your forgiveness is that I'm crazy in love with you. So crazy it makes me do crazy things. I love you. And now I know I need you in my life no matter what it costs."

Her heart nearly burst with joy at his words. "I might forgive you if you promise to never worry about either of our reputations again."

"I do promise. I've come to realize that having a spotless reputation doesn't mean much unless you have the respect of the person you love." He gave her another soft kiss. "But I've decided to take a path that won't let tongues wag anyway. A path I considered in the past but rejected because I thought I needed everyone in the hospital to think I was great beforehand."

"What path are you talking about?"

"Nick and I are going to start a private surgical practice. It will take a lot of work, but the benefits will be worth it."

She frowned. Surely he wasn't doing something so extreme just so they wouldn't have to work together? "Why?"

"He wants more control over his schedule and his life, and I want the same thing. I'm not doing it just for us, Katy, I promise, though I would if I had to. But it does take that worry out of the equation."

"And no more playing God?"

He signed an X on his chest. "Cross my heart."

"Then I forgive you. And I love you too. So much."

He pulled her close and pressed his forehead

to hers. "Thank you," he whispered. "For loving me back and forgiving my stupidity. What can I do to make it up to you?"

"I think we should get started on those goals we talked about." Just the thought made her breathless. "The one involving excitement and sailing and you kissing me all over."

"Goals are good things to have." A gleam filled his eyes and a slow smile curved his lips. "Must be fate that we're already on the boat, as I'm more than ready to get started on our first goal. Then work on a list of others that will take a long time to achieve."

"Any thoughts on new ones?"

"Yes. I know exactly what the first goal should be. Well, the first one after the other first one."

She had to laugh. "All right, what is it?"

"A big Greek wedding starring Dr. Katherine Pappas." He drew back an inch, and his gaze grew both serious and tender. "Will you marry me, Katy? I think maybe I loved you all those years ago when you were conducting weird science experiments, and insisting on helping Nick and me build a tree house, and even when you out-fished us with some special bait you'd come up with. But I'm absolutely sure I'm totally in love with you now, and I want to spend every day of the rest of my life with you."

Her heart swelled to bursting at his words, but before she could speak his lips touched hers with the sweetest of kisses.

The eyes gazing into hers weren't amber or tiger eye but gleamed like polished gold, precious and dazzling. "Will you marry me? Please, say yes."

"Yes." The easy answer barely squeezed past the lump in her throat. "Yes, I will, Alec Armstrong."

"Thank you." His arms wrapped around her and he caught her close against him. "How fast can a Greek wedding be pulled together?"

"Not very fast, but we'll see what we can do to expedite the process." She hugged him and whispered in his ear. "You do realize you'll have to practice Greek dancing."

"I might have to fake it. But one thing I'll never have to fake is how in love I am with you."

* * * * *

MILLS & BOON®
Large Print Medical

May

PLAYING THE PLAYBOY'S SWEETHEART	Carol Marinelli
UNWRAPPING HER ITALIAN DOC	Carol Marinelli
A DOCTOR BY DAY...	Emily Forbes
TAMED BY THE RENEGADE	Emily Forbes
A LITTLE CHRISTMAS MAGIC	Alison Roberts
CHRISTMAS WITH THE MAVERICK MILLIONAIRE	Scarlet Wilson

June

MIDWIFE'S CHRISTMAS PROPOSAL	Fiona McArthur
MIDWIFE'S MISTLETOE BABY	Fiona McArthur
A BABY ON HER CHRISTMAS LIST	Louisa George
A FAMILY THIS CHRISTMAS	Sue MacKay
FALLING FOR DR DECEMBER	Susanne Hampton
SNOWBOUND WITH THE SURGEON	Annie Claydon

July

HOW TO FIND A MAN IN FIVE DATES	Tina Beckett
BREAKING HER NO-DATING RULE	Amalie Berlin
IT HAPPENED ONE NIGHT SHIFT	Amy Andrews
TAMED BY HER ARMY DOC'S TOUCH	Lucy Ryder
A CHILD TO BIND THEM	Lucy Clark
THE BABY THAT CHANGED HER LIFE	Louisa Heaton

MILLS & BOON®
Large Print Medical

August

A DATE WITH HER VALENTINE DOC	Melanie Milburne
IT HAPPENED IN PARIS...	Robin Gianna
THE SHEIKH DOCTOR'S BRIDE	Meredith Webber
TEMPTATION IN PARADISE	Joanna Neil
A BABY TO HEAL THEIR HEARTS	Kate Hardy
THE SURGEON'S BABY SECRET	Amber McKenzie

September

BABY TWINS TO BIND THEM	Carol Marinelli
THE FIREFIGHTER TO HEAL HER HEART	Annie O'Neil
TORTURED BY HER TOUCH	Dianne Drake
IT HAPPENED IN VEGAS	Amy Ruttan
THE FAMILY SHE NEEDS	Sue MacKay
A FATHER FOR POPPY	Abigail Gordon

October

JUST ONE NIGHT?	Carol Marinelli
MEANT-TO-BE FAMILY	Marion Lennox
THE SOLDIER SHE COULD NEVER FORGET	Tina Beckett
THE DOCTOR'S REDEMPTION	Susan Carlisle
WANTED: PARENTS FOR A BABY!	Laura Iding
HIS PERFECT BRIDE?	Louisa Heaton